EMBERS

COMMON LAW BOOK TWO

Kate Sherwood

RIPTIDE PUBLISHING

Riptide Publishing
PO Box 1537
Burnsville, NC 28714
www.riptidepublishing.com

Embers

Cover art: Natasha Snow, natashasnowdesigns.com
Editor: Carole-ann Galloway
Layout: L.C. Chase, lcchase.com/design.htm

ISBN: 978-1-62649-530-2

First edition
February, 2017

Also available in ebook:
ISBN: 978-1-62649-529-6

EMBERS

COMMON LAW BOOK TWO

Kate Sherwood

RIPTIDE PUBLISHING

TABLE OF
CONTENTS

CHAPTER 1

Jericho Crewe was writing a ticket for underage alcohol consumption when he saw the massive flash reflected in the warehouse windows behind the drunk teenagers. His body reacted without thought, pushing the two kids to the ground in the shelter of the parked patrol car. He was crouching behind the same vehicle when the boom of the explosion reached them, strong enough to rattle the windows that had been his mirror a moment before.

"Drink at home," Jericho said quickly, shoving the ticket book back into his belt and heading for the driver's door of the cruiser. "Or don't drink at all. Whatever." It was four o'clock on a Monday morning, so really the kids should be asleep, getting ready for a fun and educational day at school, but he had bigger things to worry about, suddenly. "You two can get home safely? No driving?"

"I live just across the field," the girl said, gesturing at a row of houses on the far side of a narrow strip of land. She seemed dazed by more than alcohol. "Andy's staying at my place."

Great, so teen drunkenness can slide into teen pregnancy. A more prudish-than-expected inner voice, but not something Jericho could worry about right then. "Okay. Be safe."

He was halfway into his sheriff's department cruiser when Andy yelled after him, "Deputy Crewe! Hey!"

Jericho turned around, and the kids were both staring at him. "What *was* that?" Andy asked, gesturing in the direction of the explosion.

"Police business," Jericho said seriously. "Get indoors, and stay there."

Andy looked like he might be thinking about defying that instruction, but the girl had better sense and tugged on his hand. "Let's go."

"I see you out again tonight," Jericho said, "I'll finish writing those tickets, and see if I can't figure out a couple other charges to add to them. Go home."

There. That was the *protect* part of the job taken care of. Now he could to do something more interesting.

In the month since he'd started at the sheriff's office, Jericho had spent most of his time helping Kayla look into corruption and wading through the bureaucratic bullshit that was part of running the department. Cooperating with the FBI as they investigated his shooting of their rogue agents and all the events that had led up to that, then endless hours of poring over old arrest reports, case notes and evidence chain-of-custody paperwork had bored him so completely that the occasional night of filling in on patrol seemed like an exciting adventure. The town of Mosely didn't have its own police force, so the sheriff's department covered the little grid of houses and businesses as well as the vast rural area beyond. Town was the most likely spot to find something happening on a night patrol, and Jericho had been pretty happy to discover a couple of drunk kids to cut the tedium. But writing tickets was nothing compared to explosions. He grinned as he called in to central dispatch and requested firefighters and extra police. This was more like it.

His excitement turned into something else, something cold and tight in his belly, as he drew closer to the flames licking the night sky and realized just which building was on fire. This wasn't a fun adventure, it was a dangerous situation. Someone might have been killed if they'd been caught in that blast.

He parked the cruiser across the road to block any oncoming traffic. He was the first person on the scene, as far as he could tell, so there was no one to see him as he jumped out of the car and ran toward the burning building. The heat was too intense for him to get much closer than the edge of the parking lot.

He stood there and stared, barely aware of the churning in his stomach and the cold sweat on his skin. The building blazing in front of him was Kelly's, the bar owned by Wade Granger. And if Wade had been inside when the building exploded, there was no way he could have survived.

Jericho still had Wade's cell number, and he fumbled with his phone and stabbed at the screen, sending a silent prayer to anyone who might be listening, anyone who might care, as he waited for the number to connect.

When Wade's voice mail clicked in, Jericho wanted to scream in frustration. Instead he said, "Wade, it's Jericho. There's a problem at the bar. Give me a call as soon as you can, okay? As soon as you get this message. Call me. Now."

It wasn't enough. Jericho wanted to spill his soul, confess to everything he'd felt over the years, and everything he *hadn't* felt when he'd been with anyone but Wade. He wanted to set it all straight, stop wasting time, stop fighting something that could never be beaten. But if Wade had been in that building, it was too late for any of that.

So Jericho shoved his phone back in his jacket pocket and tried to focus on his job. His hands were shaking a little as he unrolled the crime-scene tape, but by the time the volunteer fire fighters started arriving, he was under better control.

He even managed not to punch the young asshole who sneered at the remains of the bar and said, "You want us to take it slow? No point risking our lives for scumbags like that, right?"

"Follow your standard procedure," Jericho growled, and then stalked away before the kid said anything else.

It was hypocritical to judge the firefighter. He'd been pretty gleeful himself on the drive over, until he realized whose property was involved. And first responders often developed a sort of black humor as a way to deal with the trauma of their jobs. It was Jericho's reaction that was unusual, not the kid's.

He checked his phone, then stared at the flames. They were starting to die down on their own and the firefighters seemed to be spending most of their time on the nearby buildings, making sure the fire didn't spread. Apparently they'd given up on salvaging anything from the bar. Anything, anyone . . .

Jericho's phone vibrated in his hand, and he flipped it around to see the screen so fast he almost dropped it. The last texts between him and Wade had come from Jericho's side, sending information about where his kidnapped half siblings were being held. Now the message came in the opposite direction.

Building is empty. No need for heroics.

Jericho stared at the screen. There was no emotion in the text. And he hadn't mentioned a fire, or any other reason anyone might have been contemplating "heroics." It didn't seem as if Jericho's call had surprised Wade at all. Did that mean Wade had— Had he known what was happening? Had he *planned* this? Most of Wade's criminal activity involved smuggling things back and forth across the Canadian border, but maybe he'd branched out into insurance fraud. *Maybe he's branched out into murder*, an inner voice prompted. *Maybe he killed your father. Remember that, Junior?*

Now Wade had sent a possibly incriminating message to the county Under-sheriff. Was he just assuming Jericho would keep his mouth shut about it?

No. Wade wouldn't assume anything. And he wasn't careless.

It was another one of Wade's games. Another test, another trap. He wanted to see what Jericho would do. It was simple and easy, for Wade. Tap a few words into a phone and sit back and smirk as Jericho tortured himself. Damn it.

Jericho turned away from the flames in disgust. Amazing how quickly his cold fear had turned to hot anger. His body was still shaking as if it hadn't realized that the temperature had changed. Wade didn't care about Jericho's career, didn't care about his personal ethics; he wanted to stir things up. Just like he always had. As kids, they'd taken turns being the instigator, each pushing the other's buttons and watching the ensuing fireworks, but Jericho had grown up, damn it.

He saw the flashing cruiser lights before he saw the car itself. Kayla pulled up next to him, climbed out of the driver's seat, and stared at the remains of the building, then at Jericho. He walked a little closer.

"Did anybody get out?" she asked cautiously.

He offered her his phone, showing her the message from Wade. She raised an eyebrow after she'd read it. "He knew it was going to burn?"

"Seems like."

"Insurance? He should be keeping his mouth shut. Not like him to blab."

Jericho didn't bother passing his theory about Wade's motives along. There was no point. He'd shown her the text, so his job was done.

At least that part of it. There were regular police duties to take care of: supporting the firefighters, controlling the growing number of spectators, and of course, making sure the scene was preserved so evidence could be gathered once it was safe. Evidence. Because this was probably a crime scene. And, one way or another, Wade Granger was involved.

Jericho could still smell smoke when he woke early the next afternoon. He'd showered when he got back to his apartment, but apparently that hadn't been enough to rid himself of the stench. It was likely his clothes that were stinking the place up, but he couldn't get over the feeling that the smoke had somehow seeped into his pores. After all, it was Wade's smoke, and Wade wasn't easy to escape from.

He showered again, threw his old clothes into the compact washing machine in the kitchen part of the large main room, pulled on a clean uniform, and grimaced at the beige polyester. After eight years in the Marines and five as a patrol cop, surely he'd paid his dues? Coming back to Mosely had seemed like a time warp in so many ways, and stepping back into uniform was one of the most annoying.

Still, he took a moment to give himself a quick once-over in the cheap mirror on the back of the bathroom door. He was representing Kayla, and her life was complicated enough without having to worry about her officers looking sloppy.

But when he got to the sheriff's station, it was clear that no one was going to be paying much attention to him. "Jesus," he muttered, and frowned at Deb, the middle-aged woman who ran the reception area with a precision the Marines would have envied. "They're back?"

"Just DEA so far. But depending on what started the fire last night, we might see ATF. And I wouldn't be surprised if the FBI showed up too—they were all pretty chummy last time around."

"Yeah, chummy enough to get dirty together."

"That's probably not a good ice breaker," she said helpfully. "Especially since you shot three of their guys when they were here before."

"That was justified."

"Have they had the hearing already? I hadn't realized." He stared at her and she raised an eyebrow. "You *know* it was justified. I *believe* it was justified. The feds? They may be a little further along the path from certainty."

"Damn it, Deb, do you think I need to be hearing that?"

"I absolutely think you need to be hearing it. Ideally, you would have thought of it for yourself, but that didn't seem like a level of self-discipline I could count on."

He frowned at her. They probably hadn't had a real conversation since he'd joined the department, and he wasn't really enjoying the change. "Is there a problem? You and me? Is there— Have I done something to offend you?"

Her smile was quick, warm, and real. "Not at all. But you've done something to offend *them*, and things will go better for everyone if you remember that."

"Better for—for the department. For Kayla."

She nodded. "Yes. For everyone."

It was pretty hard to argue with her on that one. "Okay. I'll keep a low profile."

"That seems unlikely. But try to be conciliatory, okay?"

"*Conciliatory*? Are you— The shootings were *justified*, Deb! They'd killed at least one man, possibly more—possibly my *father*— and they kidnapped two kids! Members of my family." They weren't exactly a *close* family, but that was none of the feds' business. "I got shot too, you know. And you want *me* to be conciliatory?"

"I want you to remember that *these* feds are not dirty. I want you to not pull out the attitude you showed the last time feds were in town. I want you to remember that Kayla doesn't need to deal with your nonsense."

And Kayla herself appeared then, distracting Jericho from trying to find out what the hell Deb knew about his so-called attitude and why she was suddenly deciding to comment on it.

"Jay, we need to talk." She strode toward him, her duty belt making her hips look wider and somehow more feminine despite their weaponry. He wondered when Kayla and Deb had formed their alliance, then remembered that *he* was Kayla's ally. Imported all the way from LA just to watch her back.

"You want to talk about the feds?" he guessed. "I already got an earful. I'm fully prepared to be professional and—" he frowned at Deb "—not 'conciliatory,' exactly, but professional. Yeah. Let's stick with that."

"That's great," Kayla said. "But not what I wanted to talk about."

"Oh."

"Come upstairs," she ordered, and he followed obediently behind her. He wished there were some feds around to see how professional he was being. And then as soon as he hit the top of the stairs, his wish came true and he couldn't remember why he'd wanted it.

"Mr. Crewe," Special Agent Hockley said. He made Jericho's name sound like a disease.

"Under-sheriff Crewe," Kayla corrected with a smooth smile. She turned to Jericho. "You remember Special Agents Hockley and Montgomery?"

Too well. They'd tried to strong-arm Jericho away from their case in the past, and from the looks on their faces they weren't any more enthusiastic about his presence now. He'd had a few optimistic moments while investigating department corruption, hoping he'd find something that would incriminate these two, but they seemed to be clean. Which didn't mean he had to like them.

But Jericho had arranged a leave from his job, moved halfway across the country, taken a pay cut, and returned to a town from which he'd barely escaped intact the first time around, all because Kayla needed someone on her side. Putting up with a couple of overentitled feds was nothing. So Jericho smiled, not widely enough to appear insincere, and nodded toward them. "Yeah, hi. Welcome back to Mosely." And then, just because he couldn't help himself: "You guys here for business or pleasure?"

Hockley frowned at him, then turned to Kayla. "As I said earlier, we'll have to discuss information-sharing protocols. I accept that we could have been more open the last time we were here; possibly that would have helped us catch on to some issues sooner. But—" he looked doubtfully, pointedly at Jericho "—there will have to be limits."

Be conciliatory, asshole, Jericho reminded himself. Still smiling, he spoke to Kayla, not either fed. "You're the boss. I've got lots to do just sorting through all the corruption stuff." He looked apologetically at Hockley. "Oh, sorry, is that a touchy subject for you?"

So much for conciliation. It was too sweet to see Hockley and Montgomery glare. But he moved on quickly. "I've been working with some good contacts at the DEA in Denver—Shelly Walton and Timothy Parsons— Oh, Shelly's the special agent *in charge* . . ." He frowned at Hockley. "I guess that'd make her your boss, huh? And she's given me full access to all her records about what's going on in Mosely. So if there's something I need, I can just get it from her instead of you. Too bad to waste her time, but, after all—there have to be limits." He turned his attention back toward Kayla. "Work for you?"

"For now," she agreed. There was a light in her eyes that might have been a warning, but he preferred to interpret it as amusement. She glanced at Hockley and Montgomery, then turned back to Jericho. "Mind if we borrow your phone for a minute?"

He raised his eyebrow. "Kay, that's a private phone. I've already shared the message with you, so I can't think of why you'd need to see it again. And if you're planning to show it to the feds—well, I'm not feeling particularly inclined to share with them right now. You know?"

"This is the sort of cooperation we can expect?" Hockley growled at Kayla. "We have to get subpoenas and search warrants for a member of your own department?"

"I'm still having some trust issues," Jericho said firmly. "After all, the last time I was involved with federal agents . . . well, let's not bring up painful memories. Although the bullet hole in my shoulder isn't exactly a memory yet, considering I just had my final physiotherapy appointment a couple days ago. But, yeah, I think it might be nice if there was a clear paper trail to show exactly what you all had access to and when. And you've got to admit—subpoenas and search warrants are a *good* paper trail."

"Jay," Kayla said quietly but firmly. "Give me your phone, please."

He could refuse, of course. It *was* his private property. If he did, though, it would make her look weak, like she didn't have control of her own people. And if he gave it to her after making a fuss about it, she would look strong and *he'd* look weak. *Damn it.* But it was Kayla, so he pulled the phone out and even went so far as to type in the password and call up the appropriate screen before handing it over. She was his boss *and* his friend.

"Thanks," she said, and held the phone up so the feds could see the screen. When Montgomery stretched to take it, she pulled it back. "It's a short message. You can just read it."

"We'd like to review the context," Hockley said.

Jericho snorted. "I was the first on the scene and called the owner of the building to get information about who might be inside. He texted that back. That's all the context there is."

Hockley's smile was almost pitying. "I think everyone knows that's not quite *all* the context between yourself and Mr. Granger."

Jericho reached out for the phone, and Kayla handed it to him without further comment. "Are we done here?" he asked her.

She made a face. "Hopefully. But, we're tight for space again, with the new arrivals . . ."

Tight for space, and Jericho was using the building's only conference room as somewhere to spread out his files. "I could work from home," he volunteered quickly. "It's not a big place, but there's a dining room table I'm not using." He grinned at her. "I wouldn't need to wear the beige if I was at home, right?"

"I'd prefer to keep you in the building," she said.

"The security of the documents is important," Hockley added. "Especially in this case."

"The security of the documents is a local matter," Kayla corrected him. "Not something you need to worry about." She stepped a little closer to the agent and lowered her voice. "And, Agent Hockley? We are *done* with you maligning the integrity of my under-sheriff. If you have any evidence of corruption or improper behavior, you can bring it to my attention. But if all you've got are sneers and innuendos? I don't want to hear them. Not to my face, and not in my building. Is that understood?"

Agent Hockley was quiet for a moment, then he nodded. "It is." He turned to Montgomery. "We should get back to work."

They walked away, Kayla and Jericho watching silently until they were out of earshot. Then Jericho said, "Sorry. I guess. I mean, possibly I could have been more conciliatory."

"They could have too." She shook her head tiredly. "My life would be a lot easier if everyone would just get along."

"If *everyone* got along, you'd be out of a job. No conflict means no cops, right?"

"I could still do traffic stops."

"Those aren't much fun."

That was when one of the deputies found them and said, "Jericho, there you are. Nikki called. She wants you to call her back as soon as you can."

"She say why?" It was unlikely that his father's widow was calling to thank him for all his help.

"Said Elijah got loose and she thinks he might be heading your way. Is Elijah her dog?"

"No," Jericho sighed. It wasn't the first time this had happened. "He's her six-year-old son." Jericho's half brother. He turned to Kayla. "He probably hasn't gone far—last time he was up a tree just a couple blocks away. But I should go deal with it."

"Yeah, you should. Maybe we can tag that kid with a transmitter, like they do with endangered animals."

It wasn't a bad idea, but it would help solve future problems, not the current one. So Jericho jogged back down the stairs he'd just come up, phone out and dialing Nikki as he moved. Getting into fights with feds and tracking down errant children: somehow, this had become his life. He glanced down at his uniform and shook his head. Yeah, it was his life, and he was living it in beige and brown.

CHAPTER 2

"I don't know why he's doing this." Nikki sounded genuinely confused, and also a little pissed off.

"How good is he at getting around?" Jericho drove and kept his gaze on the road ahead of them and the sidewalk to the left, while Nikki hopefully stayed focused on the view to the right. The last time Elijah had disappeared, he'd snuck out of his bed at night and his absence hadn't been discovered until the next morning. This time, he'd left from school in broad daylight. With any luck that would make him easier to locate, but they hadn't had much luck so far. "And do you really think he's trying to find *me*?"

"You're his *brother*." Nikki's eye roll was practically audible. "Plus, you carry a gun and boss people around and drive a car with flashing lights. You used to be a soldier." Her voice softened a little as she added, "You saved him from the bad guys."

"Wade saved him more than I did. I passed out about ten seconds after I found him."

"Yeah, he was pretty impressed with all the blood too. You're definitely his hero, at least for now."

"For now?"

"Until he realizes you're not on our side." The bite was back in her voice.

"Give it a rest, Nikki." She'd been pretty low-key when she was still in the hospital, depending on him to keep an eye on her kids in the foster home the state had found for them. But once she'd been released, her attitude had changed. He'd driven her around and helped her find a rental house on the edge of town, and he'd paid the first month's rent without even suggesting she'd have to repay him, but apparently that wasn't enough to make up for having taken the job with the sheriff's department. Jericho wasn't sure if Nikki was involved in any criminal activity herself, but she absolutely had her loyalties straight. Anyone married to Eli Crewe couldn't have cared too much about following the law; however, Nikki clearly took it a little further and considered herself some sort of desperado. It was a pain in the ass. "Let's just find Elijah."

Jericho figured he'd give it about ten more minutes before he called back to the office and got a couple of deputies on the job. Ten minutes was enough time to cover every street in the damn town. Nikki didn't want the sheriff's department involved, of course, but if Elijah was genuinely missing, Jericho needed help.

"Duck down for a minute, okay?" he said.

"What?"

"Duck down. So if Elijah looks at the car, he won't see you."

"You think he's running *away* from me?" He couldn't tell if she was hurt or angry. Possibly a combination of the two.

"Not necessarily. But he knows you'll take him back to school, or home. Right? Maybe he thinks I'll let him hang out for a while, if it's just me."

Nikki reluctantly slid lower in the seat, and when her knees hit the dashboard she slumped enough that she couldn't be seen from outside. "If someone sees me crouched down like this, next to you, they're probably going to get the wrong idea," she said, sounding pleased.

Jericho ignored her, and hit the switch to turn the flashing lights on. He wouldn't disturb the peace with the siren, especially when he wasn't really sure if Elijah would run toward or away from the noise. Hopefully the lights would attract interest without being scary. Not that Elijah had ever seemed scared of much.

Jericho drove slowly up and down the streets, trying to think like a six-year-old boy. After a few minutes he rolled the window down and caught a whiff of the pungent air; he turned the wheel and headed in a new direction.

The firefighters had soaked the remains of the bar with water, but the acrid smell was still heavy in the area, an intriguing mix of destruction and mystery. Jericho wasn't surprised to see a familiar blond head poking through the charred remains of the building. The little turkey had ignored the barricades and was conducting his own investigation.

Jericho pulled into the parking lot, and Elijah looked up, then raised a hand in casual greeting before going back to his explorations.

"Stay down another minute," Jericho said quietly. "He's here, and he's not hurt, but he's not on good footing. I want to get him out of there before he tries to run."

"This isn't about him running away from me," Nikki hissed, but she stayed crouched down.

Jericho flipped the lights off and stepped out of the car, trying to match Elijah's lack of concern. No small, uncontrollable children climbing over unstable wreckage here. No worries about dangerous chemicals or smoldering hot spots. Certainly no frustration about being dragged away from work to spend time searching for a feral brat who should have stayed at his safe, wholesome school instead of stumbling onto a crime scene and messing up evidence.

"Hey, Elijah." Jericho stood at the edge of the wreckage pile. "You need to come out now, okay? There's dangerous stuff in there. It's not a good place to play."

"There's a place that bounces," Elijah announced. He pointed, and then started moving in that direction.

"If you want to bounce, we'll find you a trampoline. But come down from there now."

"Come up with me," Elijah suggested. "You could keep me safe."

"No, that's not a good idea. It's dangerous. Come down, please."

"Are you scared?" It wasn't quite a taunt, not exactly a dare, but there was enough of both in the tone to have Jericho's inner child leaping to the challenge, ready to climb.

"I'm scared for you, yeah. I don't want to see you get hurt."

Elijah turned away as if considering Jericho's words, then stepped forward and started bouncing.

"Elijah!"

No response. Apparently the area wasn't just bouncy, it also had an invisible soundproof barrier.

Jericho was this kid's hero? Yeah, right. He glanced back toward the car, saw Nikki peeking over the dashboard, and shrugged obviously enough for her to see. He was out of ideas. He could climb up and grab the kid, but the wreckage *was* unstable, and places that might handle the kid's weight wouldn't necessarily carry Jericho's. Pretty ironic if his attempts to save the kid ended up getting them both hurt.

"Elijah!" Nikki's voice was loud. Not fearful, just angry. "Get off there right now. You need to get back to school! I've had enough of this!"

But the soundproofing evidently worked against Nikki's voice too. Elijah didn't even turn his head.

"Get him down!" Nikki ordered Jericho.

"Great idea. Got any suggestions on *how* to get him down?"

"Just climb up there and grab him," she said scornfully. "What, have you been reading child-raising books? You think you need to *reason* with him and give him the opportunity to correct his own behavior? Ignore that bullshit and get my kid off that garbage and back to school!"

It would be so easy to sever this relationship. Nikki was . . . difficult. That was the most charitable way to describe her. He'd helped her enough, surely. She might be his father's widow, but she'd never been his mother. The kids were animals, wild and ungrateful and usually surly. His life would be a hell of a lot easier without any of them in it.

Then Elijah turned his head, just a half inch, enough to get a quick glimpse of what Jericho was going to do. And there was something in the movement, some mix of tentative bravado and desperate desire to be noticed, that pulled at Jericho. Something he recognized all too well. He couldn't walk away from the kids, because they were in the same place he'd been in after his mother had died, and he'd needed someone to help him out and care about him then, although he hadn't been able to admit it.

"I'm worried about you, Elijah," he said. The boy slowed his bouncing, at least a little. "I really want you to be safe. I want you to have fun, but I'd hate it if you got hurt."

"Just grab him," Nikki said tiredly. "I swear, I'd thought a Marine would be a bit more interested in discipline." She raised her voice. "You've got about three seconds to get your ass down here, boy. If I have to climb up and get you, there's gonna be a whupping coming your way."

Elijah turned away and bounced a bit harder. Apparently if he was going to get whupped, he'd make the crime worthwhile.

That was when a new voice entered the exchange. "Hey." It was male, authoritative without being pompous, and even with one word, enough for Jericho's body to recognize it and respond. "Hey, Elijah."

Elijah swiveled his head to see the new arrival, and Jericho let himself do the same. Wade didn't bother to look toward the adults, just stared at the boy. "That's *my* pile of wreckage you're messing up," he said firmly. "Get the hell off. Now."

There was a part of Jericho that wanted Elijah to respond to this new order the same way he'd responded to the earlier ones. A part of him that wanted at least one person in the world to be immune to Wade's effortless charisma. But Elijah immediately started picking a path down off the rubble, like a tiny robot programmed to respond to only his master's voice.

"Don't suppose you're looking for babysitting work?" Jericho asked, and Wade smiled. Damn it, that smile shouldn't have made Jericho's core warm. He wasn't a kid anymore, and he needed to get himself under control.

By the time Elijah was off the wreckage, Jericho had his game face back on. "Why did you leave school?" he asked as the boy approached.

Elijah shrugged, then nodded his chin toward Jericho's duty belt. "Can I shoot your gun?"

"No," Jericho said with a scowl.

Elijah turned to Wade. "Can I shoot yours?"

"I don't have a gun with me," Wade said. "Sorry. Now, you were on your way back to school, as I understand it?"

"I don't think so," Elijah said breezily. He wasn't being rebellious, just correcting Wade's misapprehension.

"Oh, you are," Nikki said. "And you will *stay there*!"

"Can I get a ride back in the police car? Can I run the sirens?"

"No," Jericho said. But it presented an interesting problem. The school was on the far side of town; Mosely wasn't big enough for that to be an unwalkable distance, at least for a healthy adult, but Elijah was young and Nikki had only recently stopped using a cane after being shot in the thigh. Giving Elijah a ride in the squad car would be a reward, but expecting him to walk back, escorted by his mother, would be a hardship.

"I can drop him off," Wade said easily. "You too, Nikki, if you'd like a ride somewhere."

"That'd be great—" Nikki started, and then she frowned as two dark sedans bounced over the rough curb into the parking lot. "What the hell? I thought the feds were gone."

Wade raised an eyebrow. "They're like fleas. You might get rid of them for a while, but they never stay away forever."

Jericho could have argued that federal officers were a hell of a lot more persistent and annoying than any fleas he'd ever encountered, but he kept his mouth shut. He saw Special Agent Hockley step out of the driver's seat of the lead car and braced himself for the sneering.

Hockley didn't take long to deliver. "You having a little family picnic, Mr. Crewe? You bring a date? Here, to a crime scene?"

"A *crime scene*?" Wade exclaimed. "What do you mean? Are you suggesting that this fire was *arson*?" He shook his head in exaggerated disbelief. "Who would do such a thing?" Then he frowned. "Wait. Do you have any actual *evidence* to support that claim, or are you just throwing words around?"

"Mr. Granger, I'd be happy to discuss this all with you if you'd care to accompany me to the sheriff's station."

"Are *you* investigating this?" Wade asked, continuing with his innocent confusion. "Is arson a DEA issue, now?"

"We wouldn't have to limit our conversation to this issue," Hockley said calmly. Jericho was tempted to back away, leaving these two to their competition, but he really wanted to see how it would end.

"Oh, that's generous of you," Wade drawled. The more slowly he talked, the more annoying he was, and he clearly knew it. "But I actually have a very busy day scheduled. As you can imagine, losing property like this is a disruption to my business. But I would like to hear a report on your investigation, just as soon as you have— well, as soon as you have anything more than your typical fed bullshit."

Hockley nodded as if he'd expected nothing less. "I'm sure we'll be able to get this figured out without your assistance. Mr. Crewe was kind enough to share your earlier text with us, so that gives us an idea where to start."

"It does?" Wade asked. Jericho's stomach churned, waiting to see Wade's reaction now that he knew Jericho had shared that information, but Wade didn't even glance in his direction. "I can't imagine how. But okay, then. You know what you're doing, I know what I'm doing. Let's both just get on with it." He turned to Nikki, his gracious smile oozing Southern charm rather than northern reserve, and swept an arm toward his waiting pickup. "Ready to go?"

"Absolutely. Elijah, move it."

All three of them swept away in a tight unit, and Jericho should have felt relieved to see his complications leaving him. When Elijah was passing the feds he reached a small, soft hand toward Hockley's sidearm, and it was Wade who smoothly caught the boy's arm and directed him away.

"What a nice family," Hockley said, shifting around to stand beside Jericho and watch Wade help settle Elijah in the backseat of the pickup. "We've been wondering if Granger was looking to step into your father's shoes, but I admit, we were thinking of it more in a business sense."

Jericho had no time for this. "I guess he's got more versatility than you give him credit for." He started for his patrol car, but wasn't too surprised when Hockley stepped in front of him.

"I'd like to know what the hell you were doing out here, meeting with a suspect at the scene of the damn crime."

"I'd like to know why you think this crime is yours to investigate. I'm guessing we're both going to have to talk to the sheriff to get any real answers to those questions."

"This is how you want to play it, under-sheriff? Are you refusing to cooperate with a federal investigation?"

"I'll talk to the sheriff about whether this *is* a federal investigation, and then I'll decide."

Hockley sighed, then came up with a strained smile. "We should fix this. Right? This antagonism between us, it's not productive. We should go get a beer or something after work, and get over it."

Jericho squinted at him. "Why don't we skip the beer, and just, well, just both do our jobs? I know what I'm supposed to be doing, and it hasn't got anything to do with current federal investigations. So I don't think we'll need to deal with each other at all."

"I'd like to believe that too. But it's a bit difficult, when I show up at a crime scene and see you having a friendly meeting with the prime suspect."

"You never interact with suspects? Really? Huh. Seems like you're closing off a valuable way to get information, but . . . whatever, that's your business." Jericho stepped a little closer. "But I'm getting pretty tired of you acting like I'm a dirty cop, even though you've admitted you can't find anything on me. Either I'm not dirty or you're a crappy investigator. You choose which one."

"Are you getting tired of it?" Hockley stepped a little closer and squared up. "And what are you planning to do about that?"

The man wanted Jericho to take a swing at him. He knew Jericho's background, knew his training, and even with that knowledge he still wanted Jericho to start something. Was Hockley a secret black belt, hoping for a challenge? Jericho looked at the agent's stance, the musculature that could be seen past his suit, and dismissed the idea. Hockley was just so vindictive that he was willing to take a few hits, willing to get beat up, maybe, in order to get Jericho in trouble. A silver star wouldn't be enough to get assaulting a federal officer off Jericho's record. No, Hockley wanted Jericho out, and he was ready to suffer to make it happen.

But Jericho wasn't interested in doing the guy any favors.

"What will I do about it?" he asked, and he squared off too, then leaned in a little, menacing with his height and breadth and Marine-cold stare. Then he whispered, "I may cry. I really think I might. I can feel the tears building up right now." He waited, watching Hockley slump in defeat, then smiled sweetly. "I know you don't want to make me cry, Special Agent Hockley. I know you're a kind man, deep down. Aren't you?"

Hockley sighed and stepped away. "Just stay out of my case, Mr. Crewe."

"So we're back to the same old problem. You won't tell me what your case *is*, which makes it pretty hard to stay away from it." Jericho scanned the fire scene. "And Wade was—oh, wait, sorry,

Mr. Granger—was right: arson isn't a DEA concern, not unless there's something more to it."

"Then you should assume there's more to it." Hockley nodded his chin toward Jericho's squad car. "This is ours. Off you go."

"If you're looking for work, I heard there's also a kid dealing pot at the grade school—maybe you'd like to take that over too? And Mrs. Galasso out on Derry Road is absolutely sure there's someone stealing her lettuce seedlings. Straight out of the garden each night, bold as brass. I can send you my notes on that. Could all be connected—you never know."

"I appreciate your eagerness to share. We'll let you know what we need from you." Hockley smiled blandly, and Jericho returned the expression with just as much sincerity.

And that was about all there was to say. Jericho gave both agents a jaunty wave and headed for the squad car. The feds were one more aggravation in his life, but he didn't find himself brooding over them as he drove back to the station. Instead, of course, he was thinking about Wade.

Well, not *thinking*. That suggested some sort of conscious, rational train of thought, which wasn't what Jericho was being treated to. Was it possible to be *feeling* about someone? Maybe he should be honest with himself and admit that he was *obsessing* about the man. The way he'd looked, the way he'd moved, his easy authority with Elijah, the casual defiance toward the feds. It was all—damn it, it was all *Wade*. Jericho had gone cold turkey when he'd left Mosely as a teenager, but just because he hadn't been getting his Wade fix anymore didn't mean he wasn't still an addict, underneath all the discipline he'd developed to protect himself. Now he'd let Wade back into his system, and all the old pleasure centers were being reactivated and all the old pathways were firing their enthusiastic approval. Jericho was back on the junk, and the pull was as strong as it ever had been. He couldn't deny it, so now he just needed to figure out a way to deal with it.

In the meantime, he had a job to do.

CHAPTER 3

"**W**hy isn't there someone watching the rubble at Kelly's?" Jericho asked as he stepped inside Kayla's office and shut the door behind himself.

She shook her head at him. "Don't start."

"No, I'm not starting something, I'm genuinely curious. The fire marshal hasn't made it up from Helena yet, right? So, public safety aside, we should have a deputy out there making sure evidence isn't destroyed. Shouldn't we?"

"We normally would, yes." Kayla was speaking too carefully, and Jericho squinted at her.

"The feds asked you to pull the deputy?" he said incredulously.

"'Asked' is probably a generous term to describe their instructions."

"They *told* you to pull the deputy." Jericho sank into one of the leather chairs in front of her desk. "What the hell? Why?"

"They didn't see fit to share their rationale with me."

"This is bullshit."

"It smells that way," she admitted. Then she sighed. "I don't know, maybe there's a reason for it."

"Yeah, maybe there is. They're watching the site pretty closely, I guess—rolled up fast after Wade got there." She raised an eyebrow at Wade's name, but he kept talking and she didn't interrupt. "So maybe they're doing surveillance. But the bullshit part is them not telling you what they're up to. If they want to be assholes to me? That's one thing. But to you? You're the fucking sheriff, you've been totally cooperative, and the last time they were in town you had to clean up their huge fucking mess. You're *still* not good enough to get information out of them?"

She didn't respond, and the pause told Jericho what he needed to know.

"Because of me," he said. "They're freezing you out because— Seriously? Because of me? Because I used to be close with Wade?" It was unsettling, really. Jericho had done nothing improper with Wade, nothing to compromise his sworn duties. So the feds were just being paranoid assholes, covering for their own corruption problem by accusing others of being dirty. But what if that wasn't it? What if they were actually better cops than he was giving them credit for? What if they could somehow sense Jericho's obsession? Maybe they weren't so off base wondering if he could be trusted.

He'd shown Wade's text message to Kayla at the earliest opportunity. He'd shared it with the feds too. He hadn't done anything wrong. Not yet.

"You can compartmentalize me away from their cases, can't you?" He kept his voice unemotional. "I'm supposed to be focusing on sorting through the corruption stuff, and on day-to-day policing, building the department back up. So you can tell the feds you've warned me off. That you won't share any information with me. They can keep you in the loop if I'm out. Right?"

"I asked you to come here because I needed someone I could trust," she said firmly. "I'm not going to turn around and stop trusting you now just because they're paranoid. They don't know how small towns work! Everyone knows everyone—it doesn't mean we all *agree* with what everyone's doing. I can get a lot of good information from people who hang out with criminals."

"But you're careful to make sure the information is only going one way. You listen to those people, but you don't *talk* to them. We can do the same thing here."

She frowned at him. "Wait. Are you telling me you and Wade are spending time together?"

He shook his head. "Not on purpose. I tracked Elijah to the fire site today, and Wade showed up. That's the first occasion I've talked to him since I started working for you. But . . ."

She sat quietly for a while, then said, "But he's still got a hold on you. After all this time . . ." It was her turn to trail off.

Jericho wished things were different. He didn't usually worry too much about his sexuality, but just then, he'd have been happy to be straight. Of his two high school partners, why did it have to be *Wade* he remained drawn to, instead of Kayla? "He's *Wade*," he said, as if that was an explanation.

She shrugged in response. "He is. And that means he's trouble. But I trust you to keep it out of the department."

He nodded, and that was the end of the conversation. He went back to poring over old records, tracing threads of corruption that had so far led only to cops who had already been discovered and were out of the department, gathering evidence for their trials, hoping he didn't find anything to implicate anyone still at work. It was tedious but important, and he wanted to do a good job for Kayla.

He spent the next couple of days on that. He lifted weights in the dingy basement of the sheriff's office after work, then jogged home, often taking detours up into the mountains, along old hiking trails he'd once known so much better. He checked in on Nikki and the kids, thought about buying Elijah a BB gun and decided against it, and through it all, he fought to keep his mind off Wade Granger.

But on Wednesday morning he arrived at the office and saw the man himself. Wade was handcuffed but smiling politely, letting Special Agent Hockley lead him to one of the interrogation rooms as if they were about to sit down for tea. As he passed Jericho he gave a pleasant nod. Always nice to see an old friend.

Jericho followed the scene with his gaze until Hockley closed the interrogation room door, then looked away to find Kayla *and* Special Agent Montgomery watching him closely. *None of my business. Can't get involved.* He nodded an acknowledgment to Kayla before returning to his own office.

But of course it wasn't that simple. Tyler Meeks, one of the new deputies hired to take the place of those under investigation, poked his nose through Jericho's doorway before Jericho had even made it behind his desk. "The FBI's coming up!" he announced. "I mean, three bodies—yeah, you'd think they might get involved—but not unless the bodies are someone special, you know?"

Jericho sat down heavily and let the words sink in. There were three bodies. And he hadn't been called. In LA, three bodies was just another night, but in Mosely County, Montana? This was big news, a big case, and Kayla hadn't been able to tell her under-sheriff about it because she'd promised the feds to keep him in the dark.

"I guess we'll find out more when they get here," he managed, trying to seem casual and unconcerned.

The deputy frowned at him. "That's all you've got? And you're just—you're still working on all that old stuff? You're not going to switch over to the hot new case? I figured— I mean, you've got a lot of experience, right? From the city?"

"The FBI have a lot of experience too. And Kayla knows what she's doing."

Meeks didn't seem convinced, but he wandered off, probably to find someone who was more excited about his news, and Jericho tried to calm his racing pulse. The feds' lack of trust had been annoying when they had been poking around a suspected arson, but now there was a triple murder, from the sound of things, and Jericho wasn't allowed to be involved.

The last time the feds had tried to shut him out, when he'd been helping Nikki find her kidnapped children, he'd just ignored them and charged on anyway. But that had been different; he'd had good reason to believe there were dirty feds involved in the crime, and he'd been on vacation from his own duties, so he hadn't felt obliged to follow procedures. *And* the victims had been his family, however unfamiliar. Now, though, he had no real justification for getting involved. Nothing but his curiosity and pride, and he owed it to Kayla to keep those under control.

So he tried to ignore the activity outside his door, tried to focus on his work, tried not to think about Wade, cocky and uncontrolled and beautiful, somehow mixed up in whatever was going on. He tried. But after about fifteen minutes of staring at his computer screen, he slammed the mouse onto the desk and shoved his chair back so hard it bounced off the wall behind him. He couldn't just sit around; he needed to *do* something.

There was an address he'd been meaning to check out. The dirty feds had gotten a search warrant for the place six months earlier, but there was no evidence of the warrant ever being executed. And the wording on the warrant affidavit was so vague it would have been thrown out of court in LA. The property wasn't a smoking gun, but an unexecuted warrant was strange enough that he should take a look at, and more importantly, it was an excuse to get the hell away from the station.

Garron had taken over from Deb at the front desk, so Jericho told the old deputy where he was going and headed off. The house was well out of town, halfway up the side of a mountain, and by the time he arrived he was wishing he'd taken the department's four-wheel drive vehicle instead of the patrol car. But a bit of bouncing around had probably been a good distraction.

The house was old, almost certainly a settler cabin that had been updated with siding sometime quite a while ago and was then left to the elements. There was no sign of power or phone lines running into the place, so he wasn't dealing with a meth shop or a grow op. The place just looked like a deserted homestead, at first glance.

But there had been tire ruts in the mud road leading to the cabin, and there was a path worn through the weeds to the front door. No signs of life right at the moment, but clearly someone was still using the place, at least occasionally.

Jericho peered down at his phone. No cell signal, but the GPS was working, and it showed that he was only a few miles from the Canadian border. No road crossings, not for a good distance in any direction, but it wouldn't be hard for someone to just walk across the invisible line, carrying whatever he wanted in his pack. Whatever someone *else* wanted, and was willing to pay for.

Jericho had his Glock drawn as he stepped out of the car, and he took a moment to listen before he started moving. There were birds chirping, some crickets—all the sounds of a peaceful forest clearing. Nothing to set off any warnings. But the hair on the back of his neck was standing up anyway. Over the years, he'd learned to trust his instincts, and they were telling him there was something wrong about this place. He turned on his phone's video recorder, then placed it in the breast pocket of his uniform, pointed so it would record roughly whatever he turned himself toward. Not ideal, but he felt better knowing there was a record of it all.

Which meant some part of him was doubtful that he'd be around to *tell* people what happened.

He should get the hell out of there and call for backup, but he couldn't stand the thought of sitting around waiting for someone to show up. Especially if it all turned out to be nothing, just his imagination playing tricks on him. They were busy with their triple murder back at the station; he could check this out himself.

He eased forward, pausing before every new step to check the angles and make sure no one was sneaking up on him. He was so focused on human threats that he almost missed the real danger. But some instinct, some buried vestige of his military training, made him glance down just as he was about to step right into the almost-invisible wire stretched across the pathway at shin-height.

Jericho froze, only his eyes moving as he traced the wire over to an old tire laid casually in the weeds. He tilted his head enough to see a glint of metal inside the rubber. Booby trap.

Yeah, he needed backup. Well, he needed a bomb squad, really. But now that he knew what he was looking for, surely he could just be careful and get a little closer?

He lifted his foot gingerly over the wire and shuffled another step toward the building. That was when he heard the distinctive clicks of a shotgun being cocked. It had come from somewhere inside the cabin, probably right by the front door. Jericho had his Glock pointed in that direction before the sound had fully registered in his brain, but there was no real target. He was completely out in the open, and the other person was under cover, sheltered by the shadows of the porch and the walls of the building. And he couldn't take cover properly, not while he was worried about traps.

Damn it. He was a sitting duck. But the person inside the cabin hadn't shot him yet. He thought for a moment, then stepped cautiously backward. Slow enough not to alarm anyone with an itchy trigger finger, foot high enough to clear the wire.

He didn't turn around, not even when he got to the car and opened the door. Somewhere inside that beat-up cabin was a person with a shotgun, almost certainly pointed toward him, and if he was going to get shot, he wanted to see it coming. He wanted to see the movement that would tell him to dodge and give him a target to fire back at.

But nothing stirred in the house, and Jericho slid into the seat, Glock still aimed in what he hoped was the right direction, and he fumbled around to get the key in the ignition with his left hand. He probably looked like an idiot, but he wasn't too worried about his dignity just then.

Once he had the car started, though, he was reluctant to leave. He tried the patrol's two-way radio, but it had no more signal than his cell phone. He'd tipped off whomever was in the cabin; by the time he got far enough back to town for his cell or the radio to work, *then* waited for backup, the person in the cabin would have had plenty of time to clean things up and get away through the forest. This wasn't LA; SWAT wasn't on constant standby.

There was no alternative. He couldn't just sit there, waiting. He couldn't try to circle around, not with the person aware of his presence. So far, the suspect and Jericho seemed to have a truce. As long as Jericho left, he wouldn't get shot. If he stuck around and tried to find another approach? The booby trap had showed that these people were dead serious about their security, and the person inside the cabin hadn't cared enough about Jericho's safety to warn him about the wire. It was tempting to think about driving a bit away and cutting back through the woods, but if there'd been a trip wire at the front door, there were probably others elsewhere, and even if he made it to the cabin, there'd still be whoever it was inside with a shotgun while he'd be outside with no cover and no backup.

So he backed out, turned around as soon as there was room, and then drove fast, his phone out in front of him the whole time, watching it for any indication that it was getting a signal. He tested the radio almost constantly too. He was ten minutes from the house but still on the single-track road, no intersections or branches, by the time he saw a bar on the phone display. He stopped the car and got out, dialed, and after too long a wait, heard Kayla's voice cutting through the static.

He gave her a quick update, repeated the parts she hadn't been able to hear, then repeated the whole thing again, keeping his eyes wide open and his gun drawn. He hadn't seen a vehicle at the cabin, but there might have been something hidden away in the back. Or the person up there might have a satellite phone or a better radio transmitter than the one in the squad car and could have sent word to someone else to come take care of the intruder.

But if the person in the cabin had wanted him dead, he'd be lying in the dirt with a shotgun hole in his chest. Damn it, he needed more information.

"I'll stay here and keep an eye on the road," he told Kayla. "I can stop anyone from coming or going in a vehicle. But we'll need bomb squad and whoever else you can think of to get us safely inside the building."

"I'm on it," she assured him. "But it's going to take a while. Don't get impatient, okay? Wait until we get there."

"Yeah," he reluctantly agreed.

So he waited. After about thirty minutes there was a helicopter buzzing around overhead, hopefully trying to track anyone who left the site, but no vehicles showed up for the better part of an hour. And when they finally did arrive, Jericho took one look at the first car in the convoy and wanted to shoot out its tires.

Hockley and Montgomery waved as they drove past him, and Kayla, in the car behind them, pulled over far enough that the other vehicles could get around her. Jericho jogged to her driver's-side window and she said, "They're taking charge," in a flat, frustrated voice.

"Why'd you even tell them about it? Jesus, it's an old search warrant, that's all! A trip wire and a shotgun, and now suddenly it's a DEA issue?"

"They say the property's been on their radar for a while. They say it's a drop spot for smuggling."

"It's three miles from the border. Drop spot is a pretty good *guess*, but if they had any actual proof, they'd have moved on it by themselves, wouldn't they?"

"You'd think so," she agreed glumly. Then she shook her head. "But they've got the resources, Jay. I'd have had to hunt around and borrow a bomb squad and SWAT guys; they just made one call, and the teams were on the way. We need their help on this."

He straightened. "Well, I'm out of here, then. Wouldn't want to contaminate their crime scene with my corruption." His skin felt too tight, and he shook his head, trying to clear his mind. "Fuck, Kay, this was part of my investigation. How the hell am I supposed to do my job if they jump in and take over whenever I find anything?" He frowned. "You don't think they're doing it on purpose, do you? Trying to cover something up? I mean, the feds *think* they've found all the corrupt agents, but they haven't closed the case yet, right? Maybe there's more dirt than we know about."

"I don't think so. I've asked around, and everyone seems to agree that these two are squeaky clean. And I know you've been digging too, hoping to find something. But there's nothing, right? I think they're just . . . feds. Of course whatever they're doing is more important than whatever anyone else is doing."

"What the fuck *are* they doing? Why'd they have Wade in there this morning? What's all this about three bodies?" He saw her expression and frowned, but didn't bother to keep the bitterness out of his voice. "Yeah. I'm not supposed to know about any of that. Sorry."

"I hate this, Jay."

"Yeah?" He shrugged. Maybe later he'd get back to seeing her as an ally, but right then she was the person who'd told the feds about a break in *his* damn case. "Better get on up there, see if there's any scraps left for you to pick up."

"We'll talk later," she promised.

"But you won't be able to say anything," he reminded her. Then he turned and headed for his squad car, and heard her pulling away behind him.

The road back to town was just as winding as it had been on the way up. Lots of switchbacks to deal with the slope, lots of sudden twists to get around rocks or other obstacles too big to go over. Jericho took his time, falling into a sort of frustrated trance.

When the bicycle shot out in front of him he swore out loud. A startled glance from the rider, and then the bike was gone, off the road, further along whatever path it had been following.

It could have been completely innocent. Just someone taking a relaxing mountain bike ride. But the quick glimpse had been enough for Jericho to recognize the rider's face, and he really didn't think Nikki was much for recreational exercise, especially when her leg was still healing from the bullet wound.

No, she'd been up on the mountain for something altogether different. And Jericho was pretty sure he knew what it had been.

CHAPTER 4

"Thanks for not shooting me." It wasn't a normal conversation starter, but it was the best Jericho had. He'd driven down the mountain, gone back to the sheriff's station, signed out, gone home and gotten changed into jeans and a work shirt, all while trying to come up with a plan, trying to talk himself into doing the smart thing and telling Kayla what he'd seen, or maybe cutting out the middle man and going straight to the feds with the information. All that effort, and still he was there at the door of Nikki's rented house, investigating on his own, and still he hadn't thought of anything better to say when Nikki answered his knock at the door.

"I don't know what you're talking about," she replied, staring him down.

"You couldn't be bothered to warn me about the trip wire, though?"

"Again, I don't know what you're talking about."

"I guess if you'd said something, I'd have recognized your voice. So, you didn't want me dead, but you didn't care enough to actually speak up and get yourself in trouble."

"You can either start making sense or you can get the hell off my porch."

She was a pretty good liar. She looked like she'd just stepped out of the shower, probably had been washing off the grime from her trip down the mountain; if he'd come over straightaway, maybe he'd have caught her riding the bike. But even if he had, it wouldn't be proof of anything but her dedication to fitness and/or a green lifestyle. No, there was nothing here strong enough for an arrest, or for a search warrant. But Jericho knew he'd seen her on the mountain, and his instincts filled in all the other gaps. "Was it Eli's Remington? If I'd kept coming up the path, would you have shot me with my own father's shotgun?"

"Okay, you're still talking crazy, so off you go. Come back when you make sense."

"I won't be coming back to pay next month's rent, I can tell you that much. If you're working with—with whoever, then you're making your own money. The ride on the gravy train is over."

She sneered at him, then scowled around herself in a display of disgust. "You think this shithole is 'the gravy train'? Seriously? I have no idea what you're talking about with all this shooting business, but as far as what you pay for goes? Paying one month's rent on this dump does *not* give you the right to make any kind of comment on what I do or how I make money. So, yeah. Off you go."

"Who are you working for, Nikki? If you cooperate, I can try to keep you out of this. We can go after the bigger fish. But if a minnow is all we've got? I guess we'll take it."

"You assume I'm not a big fish? Why, because I'm a woman?"

That gave him pause, but only for a moment. "I assume you're not a big fish because you're living in this shithole," he said. "The bastards who are behind all this? The ones pulling your strings? They're living in mansions or penthouses off in the city. They're not riding bikes down the side of a damn mountain and coming home to scrape together a meal for their kids in their two-bedroom shotgun shack."

She narrowed her eyes at him. "Everybody starts somewhere."

"Your ambition is admirable. Completely misplaced, but impressive other than that."

"I looked up how much under-sheriffs make." She said the job title like an insult. "It's on the internet. And if you don't pay my rent next month? It'll be because you can't fucking afford to, not on that salary. So don't come by here trying to lord it over me with your big career success, 'cause I know better."

It didn't quite sting, but it hit home. Jericho was making half as much in Montana as he'd made in LA. He could have stayed in the city, gone on administrative leave while they investigated his shooting of the feds, and still been paid twice as much as he was making in Montana, even if he just sat around all day. Instead he'd put most of his stuff in storage, crammed the rest into his beat-up old Mustang, and driven halfway across the continent to live in a rental about half the size of the place he'd had in LA. And it wasn't like he could claim he had great job satisfaction, either, not lately.

"So you've got a better plan?" He made it sound conciliatory. A conversation, not an interrogation.

But she just snorted. "Not a plan you'd be interested in."

"Probably not." He took half a step back. "Who's going to look after the kids while you're in jail? Have you got that sorted out? They didn't seem to fit in too well with the foster family when you were in the hospital, but you haven't got any family, do you? Have you got a plan for that?"

"Who says I'm going to jail?"

"I do." He shrugged casually. "Maybe not right away. But eventually. I mean, we both know Eli did a couple stints. And that was okay for him, parenting-wise. For one of them, my mom was still alive, and for another I was old enough to take care of myself for a few months. Wade mentioned Eli'd been back in a few years ago, and maybe more times than that since I left? And all his buddies have been in too. Not a big deal for them. Because they weren't single moms looking after two school-age kids. Be a bit of a problem for you, though, wouldn't it?"

"*Wade's* never been in jail," she said smugly.

"Wade." How did it always come back to Wade? "Is that who you're working for? Damn it, Nikki." But he wasn't angry at her. Not really. He was angry at Wade. Why the hell had he dragged Nikki into this? Or, given her personality, why had he let her push her way in? Wade knew she had kids, knew she had ties to Jericho. "The information from the thumb drive," he said, thinking out loud. "He said he needed someone to help him take advantage of all of it. Shit, Nikki, that's dangerous stuff. How many people have died because of what was on that drive?"

"They died because of the videos, and he's already given them up." She shook her head in disgust. "I have no idea why, but he did. So there's nothing dangerous anymore. Just good information."

"Contacts, routes across the border—" Jericho tried to remember what else Wade had said was on the drive. "Drop points?" he guessed.

"You got the location of that cabin off the thumb drive, and now you're using it? Was the trip wire set up already, or did you and Wade come up with that?"

"Hey, guess what, Jericho?" She leaned in a little and overenunciated the words. "I don't know what the fuck you're talking about."

"Yeah, okay," he said. He'd tried. Sort of. And she'd given him enough to know what directions to look in, if not any real evidence. "I won't take the kids long-term, but when you get arrested, give me a call and I can look out for them for a few days, until they find a better foster family."

"Fuck you! I'm not getting arrested."

"Yeah. That's what all the people in prison used to think." With that, he turned and started down the walkway.

"I wish I'd shot you," she muttered behind him, but he didn't turn around to acknowledge the words.

Instead, he headed back to the station. It felt good to be at work in plain clothes. He was off the clock, so he wasn't going to worry too much about appearances. And he thought better when he wasn't in uniform. There was something about beige polyester that made his brain sluggish.

It took him about two minutes to decide he wasn't going to share his visit with Kayla or the feds. He hadn't uncovered enough to be useful to them, and acknowledging that he'd known the person in the cabin and that she possibly hadn't shot him because she knew him would just be another reason for the feds to think he was crooked, or at least that he had ties to the wrong kind of people.

No, he wasn't going to tell anyone what he'd been up to, but he wasn't careless enough to only store his intel in his brain. He planned to stay alive and healthy enough to share as needed, but it was best to take precautions. So he took twenty minutes to type up some notes, saved them on his desktop, and emailed a copy to himself on his work account. Surely that would take care of it.

Then he gave in to temptation and jogged down the stairs to find Deputy Garron still at the front desk.

"You holding down the fort?" Jericho asked, trying to sound casual and friendly. Garron had been a deputy when Jericho had been a rebellious teenager, and their historic relationship had been based on mutual antipathy. But surely they could move past that, now. Especially since Jericho wanted the older man to give him information.

Garron just lifted an eyebrow and looked around, making it clear that the answer to Jericho's question was too obvious to bother with.

Jericho smiled. "Yeah, okay. You don't go out much anymore, do you? Out in the field. Is that by choice, or are you stuck in here?"

"Is there a reason you're asking?"

"Just making conversation."

Garron lifted the same eyebrow again, but didn't say anything. This conversation was going about as well as the one with Nikki. Time to try a different approach.

"You must be really happy to see the feds back," Jericho said with a positive smile. "You guys are a bit—not over your heads! You know what you're doing, I'm sure. There's just, well, there's some crazy stuff going on. You guys are used to dealing with break-ins, domestics, car accidents. All this drug-smuggling crap, *plus* three bodies showing up? Damn, it's a good thing the feds are here."

"You think so?" Garron didn't sound as if he was actually asking a question. "They were here for seven months last time, didn't make a single arrest."

"Okay, but last time there were complications. There were people in their agency actually acting against them. This time, though? No one could ever think Hockley and Montgomery are dirty." He waited, so hopeful of a rebuttal that he had trouble maintaining his cover, but Garron didn't give him what he wanted.

"They're too uptight to be dirty," he said dismissively. "But that doesn't mean we need them."

"Three bodies to process. We could use their crime-scene guys for that, couldn't we?"

"Three execution-style killings? The site is clean, and everybody knows it. Those guys were killed by someone smooth enough to not leave a trace."

Jericho nodded knowingly. "Well, the feds helped with the IDs, didn't they?"

"My six-year-old granddaughter could have IDed bodies with the wallets still on them." Garron frowned at Jericho for a moment, then said, "Three out-of-state wiseguys, all of them from Chicago with records as long as your arm, turn up dead here in quiet little Mosely. Larry DeMonte and his bikers are buzzing around like spring bees on crack, but they're not saying a damn thing. The feds are chasing down some decade-old drop site because they don't have any idea where else to look, and you're hanging out down here trying to pump me for information because the feds don't like your friends and have cut you out of the loop." He leaned his impressive bulk back into the wooden desk chair and raised *both* eyebrows this time. "Anything I missed, there? Anything else you think the feds would be able to help us with?"

Busted. Jericho tried his innocent smile, but Garron had clearly seen it too many times in the past to be impressed by it now. "That was a great summary," Jericho admitted.

"Next time, just ask." Garron shook his head, and if he'd been outside, he probably would have spit on the ground. "You're a punk, but you're *our* punk. The feds have no right to freeze you out, especially not when you took a fucking bullet protecting local kids from *their* fucking 'colleagues.'"

Jericho was genuinely touched, but he knew Garron would wince at any acknowledgment. So instead, he said, "Well, while you're feeling so open-minded—what did they have Wade Granger in for today? Just the insurance fraud stuff?"

"Closed-door interrogation. I don't know what that was about. But Hockley's definitely got a hard-on for busting Granger, so he'll probably be dragging him in for questioning on every damn thing that happens in this town. That's what he did last time he was here."

Jericho nodded thoughtfully. A federal agent gunning for Wade. A wise man would take it as a reason to lay low, but Wade had never been known for his wisdom. No, Wade would see it the way he saw everything else: as an opportunity. Jericho wasn't sure he wanted to discover whether Wade planned to use the situation for profit or just amusement.

"Three dead out-of-staters," he mused. As long as Garron was being cooperative, Jericho might as well take advantage. "And the bikers are agitated. Clean killings—what level are our bikers at? Do they have guys capable of pulling a tidy execution?"

Garron nodded grudgingly. "Probably. When you were here they were strictly small-time, but Larry DeMonte's ambitious. He's been pushing pretty hard, and he's done some . . . I guess you'd call them exchanges. Sending local guys to work at bigger chapters for a year or two, bringing in some outsiders to work with his locals. Something like this would be a step further than they've gone in the past, but it's more or less the direction they've been heading."

Jericho had seen notes to the same effect in the files he'd been reviewing, but it was good to confirm them with a cop who *wasn't* currently suspended or incarcerated for corruption. "Larry DeMonte. He related to Mike DeMonte?"

"Larry's the uncle. Mike's working his way up through the organization now."

Damn, another high school acquaintance on the wrong side of the law. That was what happened when a town ran out of legitimate industry. After the mines ran dry, lots of people left Mosely, but those who stuck around either fought for the few straight jobs left or found other ways to make a living.

"You have an address for Mike?" Jericho asked.

But Garron wasn't paying attention to Jericho anymore. Instead, he had turned toward the front door of the station, a wide smile on his face. Jericho didn't think he'd ever seen the man appear happy before, and turned to see what was inspiring the expression.

Retired Sherriff Donald Morgan was one of the many townsfolk who hadn't approved of Jericho back in the day, and his opinion hadn't changed in the intervening years. He'd grudgingly helped Jericho track down the kidnapped kids, but only because his daughter had prodded him into it. Now, with no kids to save and no daughter to speak up for Jericho? The man had no reason to be tolerant.

He headed for the desk and looked Jericho up and down. "You dress like that to come to work?"

Jericho made his smile bland and cheery. "Hey, Mr. Morgan, it's good to see you again. I hope you're doing well?"

Morgan raised an eyebrow at Garron, clearly inviting him to join in a sad reflection on all of Jericho's inadequacies, and Jericho knew his tentative new alliance with Garron wouldn't stand up to that sort of pressure. Jericho might be a local punk, but he was still a punk.

And there was nothing to be gained from trying to prove otherwise, not with these two.

"I'll see you later," Jericho said to Garron, then nodded at Morgan and headed for the door.

He was halfway outside when he heard Garron's voice from behind him. "Mike spends a lot of time at the clubhouse," he said, voice loud enough to make it obvious that he was talking to Jericho. "And you probably don't want to visit that location without backup and a damn good reason. But he works at Scotty Hawk's garage, and some of the boys hang out there too. You might want to check with Scotty."

Jericho nodded. He was grateful for the information, but even more impressed that Garron had given it to him in front of Morgan. Either the old sheriff's opinion of Jericho wasn't as low as it had always seemed, or Garron had ignored his former boss in order to help Jericho out. Either way, it seemed like a sign. Maybe things were finally going to start going well.

Jericho had two legitimate choices of how to spend the rest of his afternoon. He could go home, run some errands, cook a nutritious dinner, and do some laundry. Or he could go change back into the beige polyester and return to the station for a little routine staring at paperwork. Poking into a federal investigation, even peripherally, was not a good idea.

Yeah, he knew that. But his main job was sorting through old files for evidence of police corruption, and he was uncovering all sorts of things. Clues for countless ongoing cases that might have been hidden or deliberately ignored by cops who'd been working harder at concealing crimes than solving them. Quite a few of those crimes involved the motorcycle club. So he'd just be doing his job. Talking to Mike DeMonte? All in a day's work. Not his fault if the feds suspected the bikers in a triple murder. Jericho had no way of knowing who their suspects were, since he was out of the loop. He wasn't interfering; he was following his own leads. That was his story. The feds wouldn't believe him, of course, but he didn't really care.

He whistled to himself as he strode toward the parking lot. It was good to have a plan.

CHAPTER 5

For once, things seemed to be going his way, because when Jericho got to the garage, the first person he saw was Mike DeMonte peering at the dented passenger door of a flatbed truck. Older, hairier, fatter, but still clearly Mike, along with four other good-sized men, all of them wearing the cuts of the local motorcycle club. And they all saw Jericho too, and stared at him coldly as he approached: the intimidating glare of men for whom violence was a way of life. After eight years in the Marines, Jericho had his own version of that look, but didn't use it right then, not when it was five on one.

"Hey, Mike," Jericho said. They were in the front lot of the garage, in full view of the street. As long as he stayed cool, there shouldn't be any danger in the situation. Well, as long as he stayed cool and the bikers did the same. "Been a while."

Mike squinted at him. "Holy shit. Junior Crewe? That you?"

Not quite the nickname Jericho would have chosen for himself, but he managed to smile anyway. "'Fraid so," he admitted. "How've you been, man?"

They gripped forearms but didn't hug, thank god. Jericho wasn't a hugger. "Not bad," Mike said. "How 'bout you?"

"Can't complain." Jericho made sure his shoulders were relaxed and his voice easy. "You married yet? When I left you were dating . . . damn, what was her name? Blonde, curvy—"

"Careful, now. That's the mother of my children you're talking about."

"Really? Congratulations, man. How many?"

"Two boys. Eight and five."

Jericho nodded. That was useful information. He could have found it from a different source, of course, but no words on a computer screen would tell him about the proud light in Mike's eyes as he spoke about the kids. A loving father.

"You don't have any kids?" Mike asked, and when Jericho shook his head, Mike continued with, "Heard you're stepping in with Nikki's kids, though. That's good of you."

"I don't know what the fuck I'm doing."

"None of us do!" Mike laughed, then turned to the other men. "This is Eli Crewe's boy, Jericho." Mike gave Jericho a quick look, then shrugged at the men. "Junior's made a few unfortunate life choices. But as long as he doesn't go rubbing it in our faces, I think we can ignore it for old times' sake."

Jericho had the strange feeling that Mike was talking more about Jericho's sexuality than his profession, but unless the biker intel was better than he expected, that was just paranoia. Of course, Wade might have said something, but he couldn't really have exposed Jericho without outing himself. Or maybe Wade already *was* out. And damn it, there he was, thinking about Wade Granger again, this time in the middle of a goddamn investigation. "I appreciate your understanding," he said to Mike, trying to sound cool.

"Well, no, I don't think I could go all the way to saying I 'understand.'" Mike looked a bit more serious now. "I mean, your great-granddaddy and mine ran rum together, and every generation since then, Crewes have been out in the woods, crossing the border with whatever the hell they feel like carrying. Now you're back, and you're on the other side of it all?"

"I'm on the side that keeps children from getting murdered." It was a bit early to play that card, but Jericho went for it anyway. "Two local kids get grabbed and terrorized? I'm on whatever side stops that shit. Absolutely." He saw Mike's thoughtful frown, and added, "I honestly don't give a good goddamn who carries a couple cartons of cigarettes north or a couple bags of weed south. The world has bigger things to worry about. But when there starts being enough money involved for cops to go crooked, that worries me. When people start getting killed to cover shit up? That's a problem. When we've got fucking federal agents crawling up our asses and acting like they own the damn town? I don't like it."

He leaned closer. "And when we get three out-of-state assholes coming around looking for trouble, pushing hard enough that someone had to make them dead? That worries me too." He shrugged and leaned back, then smiled. "Shit, that was more of a speech than you were expecting, huh? Got a little carried away."

Mike was watching him warily, but it was one of the other men who stepped forward and said, "So what are you doing about it? Why are you here?"

"Mostly just to say hi to Mike," Jericho said, slow and casual and easy. He hoped. "But, yeah, I also wanted to make contact, I guess. I don't want to start trouble with you guys. You're local, I'm local; I just want everyone to get along. I want our kids to be safe, and I want outsiders to stop stirring shit up." He stepped back. "I figured you all might want that too. So I just wanted to come by and make that clear. I was just planning to talk to Mike, but it's good that a few others of you heard me. You all can talk it over. And if you need any help with anything, you can let me know. Okay?"

Mike gave him a careful gaze and an even-more-careful nod. No commitments, but not an absolute refusal, either. It was a step in the right direction.

So, of course, that was when the dark sedan showed up, wheeling up onto the asphalt pad in front of the garage like the occupants were Secret Service men late to protect the president. Agent Hockley stepped out from behind the wheel, Agent Montgomery from the passenger side; they both stared at Jericho, and he could feel the bikers staring at him too.

It wasn't hard to find a sullen, disinterested gaze to fix on the feds. "You looking for someone?" he asked. He was a local, they were outsiders. The bikers could trust him; the enemy of an enemy was a friend. At least he hoped that was how they'd see it.

The agents continued to stare at him. "We're in the middle of an investigation, Mr. Crewe. We'll talk to you later."

"Right," Jericho drawled. He was pretty sure he was channeling Wade's attitude. "Your work is very important."

Agent Hockley gave him a furious glare, then turned to the bikers. "We're DEA. Federal agents. We're interested in speaking to Michael Anthony DeMonte."

Nobody moved. Jericho kept his face still. Part of his brain was busy realizing that Mike's parents had made his initials M.A.D., but mostly he was trying to figure out how to play this. He wanted the bikers to think he was on their side against the feds. He didn't want to get in the way of the feds' investigation, but if they didn't even know what Mike looked like, they clearly weren't all that far into the process. Hopefully it wasn't too important for them to identify Mike right then.

So he stepped to the side, out of the scene, and waited for the bikers to draw their own conclusions.

"Michael DeMonte," Agent Hockley repeated, louder this time, in case Mike was hiding behind one of the cars in the lot.

Did the asshole not have a mug shot or surveillance photo he could have consulted? They'd just driven over expecting cooperation? Damn, that was a special kind of stupid.

The bikers were still keeping half an eye on Jericho, clearly waiting for him to point Mike out, and when he didn't, the atmosphere shifted. One of them stepped forward and said, "I could get a message to him, probably. He'll want to know what you want to talk to him about."

"You can just tell him that we want to talk to him," Hockley said. "No details needed. I'll leave you a card."

The biker grinned. "Oh, details *will* be needed. If you want to have a prayer of Mikey getting in touch with you, he'll want to know why you're interested."

"Ongoing investigation," Hockley bit out. He frowned, scanning the men in front of him. "Is one of you Scott Hawk?"

"We could get a message to him too," Mike said. His smile was nothing but polite. "You could leave *two* cards."

"And then you should sit by the phone, waiting for them to call," another biker said.

Jericho wondered what effect his own presence was having on this interaction. It was probably making the bikers more playful; they liked the clear antagonism between himself and the feds. And he was pretty sure it was making Hockley more aggressive. More frustrated.

He wasn't just appearing ineffective, he was doing it in front of Jericho, and that had to sting.

So Jericho wasn't totally surprised when Hockley growled, "I'd like to see some ID, please. From all of you."

The bikers didn't move. Jericho should have kept his mouth shut, of course, but instead he took a half step forward and reached for his wallet. "I've got my license right here—"

"Shut up, Crewe," Hockley said with a disgusted scowl. He turned back to the bikers. "I'd like to see ID from those of you I don't already know."

"I'd like a pony," Mike said calmly. "You get me a pony, we'll talk about showing you ID."

Hockley took a deep breath and exhaled it forcefully. Jericho felt like dragging the agent around the corner and yelling at him. Did he not *know* the Montana laws, or had he honestly believed he was going to be able to bluff these men? The law said he could ask for ID, but they had no obligation to provide it. And Hockley had thought members of a criminal organization wouldn't know that?

The agent squinted at Jericho. "You're going to be answering some questions for me, Crewe."

"Well, as we've just seen, you have the right to *ask* questions, Agent Hockley. I think you might be jumping to conclusions on the *answering* part."

Hockley shook his head and snarled, "Get in the car. We'll talk on the way to the station."

Jericho reacted without hesitation. "No, thanks. Why don't we talk tomorrow? You can catch me up on all the interesting news."

Another snort, more narrowed eyes, and then Hockley turned to Montgomery. "We should get out of here. We have some *real* police work to do." And that was it. They climbed back into the car.

Jericho stared at them. His reaction *had* been instinctive. He didn't respond well to authority, and definitely didn't respond well to Hockley. And the bastard knew all that. Was Hockley really that stupid, or was something else going on?

"They're as much of a pain in your ass as they are in ours," Mike commented as the agents' sedan backed out.

"More," Jericho replied. He needed to think about all this, but there was no point in blowing things with the bikers. "I have to deal with the fuckers every damn day."

"But they aren't trying to *arrest* you."

"I wouldn't be so sure." Jericho shrugged his dismissal. "But whatever. They're not the only police in town. I just wanted to come by and check in. Like I said, I'm not too worried about what locals are getting up to, but I don't like hearing about out-of-towners sniffing around, looking for trouble."

"The kind of trouble those Chicago boys found?" one of the bikers said proudly. "I don't think we need to worry about them anymore."

"Not those three, no. But usually— You guys know all this. Usually guys like that have someone behind them, backing them up. So the problem might not be solved quite yet." And the *murders* certainly weren't solved, but he didn't think he'd make a big deal about that, not with his current audience. "My salary is paid by the people of Mosely County, Montana. That's who I plan to serve and protect. So if the people of Mosely are having trouble with outsiders? I'd like to know about that." He waited for a moment, then smiled at Mike. "Say hi to your family for me, will you?"

"Yeah," Mike said, stepping forward and extending a hand. "My uncle especially, maybe?"

"Whoever you think." Jericho nodded to the other men and headed for the Mustang. Good choice to have come in plain clothes and his own car, that was for sure. But if he was going to get anywhere with the bikers, it wouldn't be because he'd dressed down for the visit. No, it would be because Hockley had shown up and displayed his usual contempt.

He mused over that for the short ride home, but when he saw the pickup parked in front of his building, his mind emptied of everything else. Wade. Not in the truck, but around. Jericho found his own parking space and started toward the front door. Wade was there. And even while his brain shouted warnings, his body moved forward.

CHAPTER 6

"**Y**ou've had a busy day," Wade said quietly as Jericho approached the apartment building. Wade was leaning against the brick wall, smiling like someone who knew secrets. Someone who knew *Jericho's* secrets.

"You too, I expect. Arrested, and all."

"Not arrested. Brought in for questioning."

"In cuffs?"

"Nothing wrong with handcuffs, Jay." Wade smiled, slow and lazy, and Jericho felt it in places he shouldn't.

He needed to maintain control of this conversation. Or at least of himself. "And you're here now because Nikki called you?"

"I'm here because I heard you were visiting old friends, and I thought maybe I could be on your list."

"You heard—" Jericho stared at him. "I *just* left the garage! You heard about that already?"

"I heard about it as soon as you arrived, Jay." Wade seemed disappointed in Jericho's slow-wittedness. "Scotty Hawk and I are tight, remember? And he called me when he saw you. Thought you were looking for me. You can imagine how disappointed I was to hear that wasn't true."

"So you came over to—what? What are we doing here, Wade?"

Wade leaned in a little, and his voice was lower than before as he said, "We can do whatever you want, Jay." Then he straightened before adding, "But we should probably do it inside? In private?"

No, they absolutely shouldn't. There was no way it was a good idea for Jericho to be anywhere private with Wade, especially not with this suggestive, seductive version of the man. So there was no reason at all for Jericho to unlock the front door of the building and push it open, leaving room for Wade to move inside.

They walked up to the second floor in silence. Jericho was more aware than he should have been of how he moved, of what Wade was seeing from his place a few steps behind. Damn it, this was a terrible idea.

And as soon as he got inside the door of his unit, he made things worse. "Beer?"

"Sure," Wade agreed absently. He was gazing around at the beige walls, the brown furniture that had come with the apartment, the almost complete lack of personalization. As Jericho twisted the lids off two bottles of beer, Wade grinned. "Damn it, Jay, this place matches your uniform. Did you plan that?"

"Lucky coincidence." Jericho handed one of the bottles over, and as Wade took it their fingers brushed. Of course they did. As if Wade would have passed up that opportunity for another little poke, another exploration of Jericho's defenses. And Wade clearly noticed how Jericho pulled away too quickly to be casual.

Wade didn't even sip his beer, but Jericho took a healthy swig of his own, and then another. He needed to cool down, but the way Wade was watching him was having the opposite effect. Jesus Christ, this was a mess, a potential disaster, and Jericho couldn't make himself do anything to stop it. He couldn't make himself *want* to stop it.

When Wade shuffled a half step closer, Jericho didn't move away. He stared at his beer bottle, took another swig, and swore at himself for acting like a hormone-addled teenager. Wade was right there, close enough to smell, close enough to practically feel the heat coming off his body, to see the stubble on his jaw and the glint in his beautiful damn eyes. But Jericho shouldn't be affected by any of that. "What do you need, Wade?" he croaked.

"Need?" Wade smiled and took his first sip of beer. He was so maddeningly controlled. This situation would be easier to accept if Jericho wasn't the only one losing his mind. And sure enough, Wade shook his head and said, "I don't need anything from you, Jay." He took a step backward then and raised his eyebrows. "Which is a good thing, or I'd have been totally fucked these last fifteen years, wouldn't I?"

There was a bite to the words, an accusation. Jericho hadn't just left Mosely; he'd left Wade, and clearly Wade hadn't forgotten that. "So, what do you *want*, then?" But maybe that was too desperate a question. "Why are you here?"

Wade took another sip of beer, and Jericho couldn't look away from his lips pursing to meet the bottle. Which meant he got to see them turn up into a patented Wade smirk. "Been a while?"

Fuck, maybe that was it. Jericho wasn't obsessed with Wade specifically, he was just horny in general. He hadn't been seeing anyone in LA, so his hookups had been a bit randomly spaced, and then Mosely was a fucking gay desert, as far as he could tell. "A while," Jericho agreed.

"Yeah, I could tell. It's like you don't know how to be a host anymore. You must have had Kayla over? Or some of your sheriff's department buddies?"

Jericho's brain stuttered for a moment, then caught up. Wade was talking about general hosting duties, not sex. At least, on the surface. That was the straw he'd laid over the pit he'd dug to trap unwary prey. Goddamn typical Wade. Jericho might not have any self-control, but surely he still had a tiny bit of pride stored away somewhere? He pulled himself together, looked Wade in the eyes, and said, "Sorry, I wasn't expecting anyone. Didn't get my baking done this week. All I've got to offer is beer."

"Don't sell yourself short. You've got lots more than that to offer."

But Jericho's pride held. "No, just beer. And a quick conversation, if there's something you wanted to say. So, was there a reason for the visit?"

Wade's sad expression was too exaggerated to be real. "I wanted to make sure you were okay. And maybe to offer a little friendly advice."

"Thanks for the concern. What's the advice?"

Wade sighed. "I'm not sure if I should give it to you, or if saying it will make you turn around and do what I say *not* to do."

"That is quite a problem you're facing. Let me know when you've got it figured out."

"I'm not sure I ever *will* have it figured out, though." Wade's smile seemed a bit more genuine now. "That's one of the things I like about you."

No, Jericho couldn't let himself fall back into the trap. "Wade. Cut to the chase."

Wade took a long swallow of his beer. "You probably already know all this. But in case you don't, or in case you're just looking at it from one perspective—there's trouble coming. Out-of-state players coming in, upsetting the bikers, trying to do business in this territory. Obviously the first battle went to the bikers, but it's not over, and the next time the out-of-staters won't underestimate their enemy. It's going to get bloody."

"And would you be willing to testify to any facts that could support this idea?" Jericho watched Wade's expression turn from incredulity to amusement. "No? Because, otherwise, you're right. I probably already knew that. What we need now is proof, ways to stop further violence, possibly by arresting and convicting anyone involved. If you can't help me with that, I'm not sure there's much else to say."

"The point of this conversation is that you don't need to be involved. You're here to clean up some police corruption. That's important work. You should stay focused on that, and leave the other stuff to the feds. Cross-border issues are their business, right? Nothing you need to be in the middle of."

"We should write this down. On this date, for the first time in history, Wade Granger agreed with federal law enforcement." Jericho set his empty bottle on the counter. "I'm not in the middle of it. The feds aren't letting me in, not at all."

"Well, if that's true, I'm very pleased. But are you sure it's true?" Wade shook his head. "Scotty told me about the little scene at the garage. The feds making it clear they have no use for you. Seems a bit unprofessional of them, doesn't it? Unless they had a reason for it."

As usual, Wade's thoughts were on the same path as Jericho's, but way the hell further along. "So what was their reason?"

"To build your cred with the bikers. To help you get deeper inside their operation, so you can report back whatever you find. But the feds are pushing the wrong guy into the job." Wade smiled fondly. "You've never been a good liar. You probably never did any undercover work, right? You're too straightforward. Too honest. It's one of your greatest weaknesses, Jay."

"I'm sure I seem honest in comparison to you and your crowd, but that doesn't mean I'm a bad liar, not compared to the rest of the world."

"But that's my point. You're not in the rest of the world, now. You're in Mosely. And you're poking your nose into the business of people who—yeah, who *are* my crowd, more or less. People like me. You've been out swimming in the ocean for way too long, and now you're crawling back into the shit and you think you're going to be able to float. But they'll—" He stopped himself. "*We'll.* We'll pull you under. And your federal friends don't care, as long as you can give them some useful intel before you drown."

"That's quite a metaphor. You thought about maybe dropping the whole life of crime and becoming a poet?"

"You thought about maybe dropping the whole law-enforcement thing and staying the fuck alive?" Wade was intense, now. Real. His eyes had caught Jericho's and wouldn't let go. "The feds are trying to get you in with the bikers. They've worked you out, and they know how hungry you are to prove them wrong. They've been poking at you, accusing you of being dirty? So you're dying to show them you're a good cop, and they know you'll take risks to make that happen. The fuckers are playing you, Jay. Absolutely."

"They're playing me to make me do my job?" Jericho tried to stay cynical and remote, but it wasn't easy. Not when everything Wade was saying fit together so well. "They don't have to do that. I would have done my job anyway."

"But your job isn't getting in tight with bikers. Is it? Your job is to help Kayla manage her department, and help her sort through all this corruption crap. The feds don't want you doing that—" He held his hands up quickly to forestall Jericho's words. "Not because they're dirty. They're not worried about what you're going to find. They just want to use you for their case, not for Kayla's."

"You think they're that manipulative? Seriously?"

"Yeah." Wade finished his beer. "I think they are. But the thing is? Manipulating you really isn't that hard. It's not a sign that they're master puppeteers or anything. You're *easy.* You wear your heart on your damn sleeve, your reactions are predictable, your damn *conscience* is practically visible to the naked eye." He stepped a little closer.

"You're a good guy. That's the problem. Being a good guy in a mess like this? It's going to get you dead."

Jericho tried to swallow. He didn't want to see himself in Wade's words, but he couldn't deny the basic truth of them. Wade had always been crafty, the perceptive one who sat back and watched and understood as Jericho flailed around. And that had been when they were just kids. In the years since, Jericho had spent all his time in jobs where he'd been required to follow orders and procedures, where thinking for himself had been generally discouraged. Even as a detective he'd worked homicide, where the crime had already been committed and all he'd had to do was prove what had happened.

Wade, on the other hand? Wade had been in Mosely, wading through shit. Figuring things out, and probably getting even better at it than he'd already been. Jericho couldn't ignore his opinion. But he couldn't trust him, either.

"You've got no ulterior motives, here? You came over as a concerned citizen, wanting to help protect a public servant?"

"I don't think of you as a nameless public servant. You know that. You can think what you want about my business, my character, any damn thing. But don't be stupid enough to think I don't care about you."

Jericho should have had a response. A defense, an attack—something. Instead, he just stood there, and so did Wade, mercifully silent for a change.

They were still staring at each other when Jericho's cell buzzed. He half turned, enough to not be looking at Wade when he answered the call.

"Crewe," he said, trying to keep his voice level.

"Are you working with the feds now?" Kayla demanded loudly enough to carry to Wade's ears. "Jesus Christ, Jay, I did not authorize this, and I don't think it's a good idea."

"Wait, what?" Jericho needed a second to catch up. Wade's theorizing was one thing, but Kayla was talking like it was already accepted fact. He tried to form a coherent response. "I don't know what they're up to. I didn't agree to anything. They're—" Well, it was stupid to try to deny it. "They're playing some game, yeah. But you're my boss. I work for you, not them."

"You're goddamn right you do." She sighed. "Okay. So if I go yell at them for involving my under-sheriff without my permission, they're not going to have any comeback for that? They can't make it about me not having proper control over my department?"

Jericho tried to put himself into Hockley's mindset. It was a creepy place to be. He thought back to the confrontation at the fire site, the way Hockley had been pushing for a fight. Pushing, or testing Jericho? "They might say I involved myself by poking my nose into their business. But again, I can't know what their business *is* without them telling me. They never explicitly said to stay away from Scotty Hawk's place or the bikers."

"Yeah." Then she added, "Look, if they've already done this, I can maybe use it. Do you want me to? Like, should I say that they'd better not do it again, but what's done is done, and you'll go along with whatever they're planning, as long as they let you right into the investigation. If you want, I can say they can go ahead, as long as you're a partner, not a pawn. Do you want me to do that?"

Jericho knew Wade was probably right. He wasn't made for this sort of delicate situation, hadn't learned to interpret and use the subtle shifts in Mosely criminal power. He was in over his head, and didn't know how to swim. At least, not how to swim in shit. Still, he said, "Yeah. If you can do that, it'd be great. I want in."

"No promises, but I'll see if I can work something out," she said. "Talk to me tomorrow morning, first thing, and I'll tell you where we are."

She hung up, then, and Jericho turned around. Wade set his bottle down carefully on the counter. "You're not making it easy to keep you alive," he said mildly.

"It's not your job to keep me alive."

"It doesn't seem to be anyone else's, either."

"I did four tours in Afghanistan, and was a beat cop for five years in a pretty rough neighborhood. I can take care of myself."

Wade shook his head sadly. "That attitude right there? That's what worries me." He shrugged and headed for the door. "I'll do what I can. But you could help me out a little, couldn't you?"

"By sitting around doing paperwork all day?"

"That would be super, yeah." He turned back with his hand on the doorknob. "Hockley and Montgomery are clean. They're assholes and they'll use you without hesitation, but they're clean cops. Mike DeMonte's a fucking psychopath—he can play nice when he feels like, seems like a good ol' boy, but don't trust him. Not at all. His uncle's almost as bad. The two of them are the ambitious ones in the club, and they're the only ones with any serious brains. As for the guys coming in from out of state? I don't know as much about them, obviously, but they're the real deal. Ties to a Chicago organization run by a guy named Anders Pilman, from what I'm hearing. You should look him up, maybe."

Jericho stared. If the information was accurate, it was valuable. Too valuable for Wade to be sharing for free. "And how do you fit into all this?"

"Me? Fuck, Jay, I'm a little fish trying to stay out of the way of the sharks. Just like *you* should be. I don't fit in at all." He left then, pulling the door shut gently behind him.

Wade wasn't involved in any of this? That was pretty hard to believe. Maybe the feds would be able to tell Jericho differently, if Kayla persuaded them to talk to him. Or maybe they'd make him believe Wade was telling the truth. He had no idea which result to hope for.

CHAPTER 7

The next morning, back in brown on beige, Jericho sat in the station conference room with Kayla, Hockley, and Montgomery. Kayla had brought him there after they'd talked in her office. Apparently Jericho was in, at least nominally.

But he wasn't sure he believed it. "So why'd you change your mind about this?" he asked Hockley.

Hockley shrugged. "You did good work with that drop house. We saw the video you took . . . you kept your head. And the sheriff insists that you can be trusted."

"That's all? Because Kayla's been saying all along that I can be trusted, and what happened at the drop house was more frustrating than dangerous."

"We're short-handed. We assessed our possible resources and decided to take a chance. Now, was our chance worth it? Do you have anything to add to the investigation?"

There was something going on, something Jericho didn't like. Didn't trust. "You've been playing me the whole time," he said. "All your bullshit—that territorial crap when I first got here, being an asshole at the fire, all the pushing and poking—it's all been an act."

"No," Montgomery interjected. "He really *is* an asshole."

Hockley gave his partner a quick, unreadable look, then smiled tightly at Jericho. "You and I approach situations differently. You apparently operate on instinct, while I prefer a more intellectual approach. So, yes, I've been trying to figure you out, trying to understand you and come up with the best way to use you."

"*Use me*," Jericho echoed. "You're that upfront about it?"

"You're a law enforcement officer. A resource. Would you prefer 'utilize' or 'activate'? I'm not too concerned about what word we use."

It was too close to Wade's assessment, not only of the situation and the feds' goals, but also of Jericho's damn character. He was starting to feel like an ignorant child being manipulated by everyone around him. But if he objected, he'd feel like a *petulant* ignorant child. So he shrugged and said, "I'll take a look at what you've got and see what holes I can fill."

Hockley nodded. "We can go over our notes. But short form? We're here to deal with the porous border, in general. Currently, though, we've been distracted by a triple murder. Execution-style. The victims were from out of town."

Yeah, Jericho had gotten that much from Garron. "Their wallets were still on them, right? So you've got names?"

They did, but not much else. At least, not much that they bothered to share in their terse summary of the situation. Well, what the hell, Jericho could make a show of good faith and see if it got him anywhere. "I've heard there's a connection to an organization based in Chicago, headed by a guy named Anders Pilman. Has that name come up at all?"

Hockley leaned forward. "The bikers told you that?"

Shit. "No. Wade Granger did."

"Wade Granger." Hockley let the name hang in the room for a while before saying, "This just came up in casual conversation?"

"I don't think Wade's ever had a casual conversation in his whole life. He came to my place last night, told me I should stay out of things. When I made it clear I probably wouldn't be doing that, he said the DeMontes are psychos and shouldn't be trusted, and gave me that name for the other side of the turf war."

"That's how he characterized the situation? A 'turf war'?"

"I don't think he used that phrase, but that was the idea, yeah."

"And why do you think Mr. Granger passed this information along to you?" Hockley's voice was light, but his gaze was sharp.

"I assume he wanted me to pass it along to you. He already tested me with the text about the bar, so he knew you'd end up hearing about this. But why he wanted you to have the information? I have no idea."

"He certainly hasn't been too forthcoming in *our* conversations with him," Montgomery said.

"Most of your 'conversations' are interrogations, aren't they? Handcuffs are involved? That's not going to work. You're not going to intimidate Wade into any damn thing."

"Sounds like you admire him for that." Hockley was still prodding, still playing his game, but Jericho was on to him now.

"A bit more intel from him, in case you're interested." Jericho leaned back in his chair. "He said you two were assholes. Clean, but . . . assholes." He glanced at Kayla, then back at Hockley. "I assume he meant for me to pass *that* along, as well."

"We've probably come to the end of any useful intel here," Kayla said firmly. "Hockley, you'll use your resources to investigate that name? Anders Pilman? Jay, you'll review the federal files and see if you've got any additions or comments? And if the bikers contact you, you'll come to us before you take action. Right?"

"That can be my goal," Jericho said. "Can't guarantee it'll be possible, of course."

"Make it happen," Kayla said. "Wade was correct about the DeMontes being psychos, and they've got a well-armed crew. If I'd known about the little stunt yesterday," and she shot a dirty look toward the feds, "I would have vetoed it. We are *not* setting you up to seem like an ally of the bikers, and you are *not* authorized for any more of your solo cowboy bullshit." She sighed. "If they contact you, let us know. Otherwise, leave them the hell alone."

"We're running scared?" Jericho asked. "The bikers can do whatever they want because we're afraid to get in their way?"

"If we decide to get in their way, we'll do it," Kayla corrected. "But we'll do it smart, and we'll be prepared. It will be a tactical strike, not you blundering around and poking at people until somebody pokes back."

Well, that wasn't exactly how Jericho would have characterized his investigative technique, but he couldn't really come up with a strong rebuttal. "If they poke back hard enough, they could expose themselves and give us something we could use."

"If they poke back hard enough, you'll be dead," Kayla retorted.

"You and Wade should get together and have drinks, sometime. You might find you've got more in common than you think."

Hockley broke in. "Are you saying that Mr. Granger threatened your life?"

Jericho sighed. "No." He grabbed the folder and stood up. "Okay. I'll look through this. I'll let you know if the bikers contact me."

Kayla nodded a dismissal, and he left the other three in the conference room. He was in his office a few minutes later when Kayla came in and shut the door behind her.

"What's going on with Wade, Jay? I mean, is this going to an ongoing thing, him visiting you at home?"

He frowned. "You asking for yourself, or for the feds?"

"Damn it, I'm asking for *you*! You need to be careful of him." She took a deep breath. "Look, I know you and Wade used to be close. I get that. But you're not kids now. You're playing a dangerous game if you're having anything to do with Wade Granger."

"Jesus, Kay, he saved my life a month ago! Risked his own skin to do it."

"You think he got involved just to help you out? You think he wasn't sniffing around for that thumb drive, looking for an opportunity the whole time?"

"He sent you the video. The clip that allowed you to figure out who was dirty in your department *and* that's going to help convict them and the feds. What was his ulterior motive for that?"

"I don't know, but that doesn't mean he doesn't have one." She frowned at Jericho for a moment, then more quietly said, "When you left Mosely? I was sad for myself, and I knew I'd miss you. But I was so *fucking* glad you went, all the same. Not just because you needed to get away from this town, but because you needed to get away from Wade fucking Granger. I could see—*everyone* could see—that he was going to drag you down. You had a chance to get away from that, and you took it, and it was the smartest thing you've ever done."

She waited as if to allow him to object, but he couldn't. She shook her head. "And now you're back. I know, I'm the one who made that happen, but you know what? I thought you'd have learned. I thought you'd gotten out in the world and had enough experiences to realize how *healthy* people behave, and I thought you'd come back with some common sense. But what the hell am I seeing? You're running back to him like a magnet heading for the north pole!"

Jericho frowned. "Magnets don't actually—they don't travel north, Kay. Not under their own power. Magnets don't *migrate*."

"Shut up. You know what I mean."

Yeah, he did. He looked out the window as he said, "I didn't know Wade was going to be at my place. He invited himself in. I gave him a beer, he tried to convince me to stay out of whatever's going on between the bikers and the out-of-staters, and he left. That's all. He was in the building for maybe ten minutes."

"He tried to convince you to stay out of it," she said thoughtfully. "Why?"

"Well, he didn't use the exact words, but the gist was that I was going to get killed if I wandered around poking at people until they poked me back. Sound familiar?"

"What's his angle? What's he trying to achieve?"

"Shit, you think I know? I mean, is he actually trying to get me to stay out of things, or is it some sort of reverse psychology and he actually wants me *more* involved, or is it really a double psych-out where he wants me to *think* it's reverse psychology? Any of that is totally possible."

"Yeah. Any of that and more." They were both silent for a while, and then Kayla shrugged and opened the door. "So it's important for you to keep me in the loop. Clear?"

He nodded. "Okay. Communication. Got it."

"And try to stay away from Wade. I mean it. Making a deal with the devil rarely works out for anyone but the devil."

He let her leave without arguing, but as he sat there and stared at the paperwork in front of him, he knew he didn't believe her, not in his heart. Wade wasn't the devil. He was . . . devil*ish*, maybe. Certainly not an angel, except maybe of the fallen variety. But being a devil, being *evil*, that was clear and straightforward, and there was nothing straightforward about Wade Granger.

Jericho kept his mind on his job, going through the feds' files and making a list of notes and questions, until his cell phone rang around lunchtime. A glance at the call display had his shoulders tensing, and he answered with, "Hi, Nikki. How do you plan to complicate my life today?"

"That's charming. A really nice way to talk to family."

"You going to answer the question?"

She was quiet for long enough that he pulled the phone away from his ear to see if she'd hung up, but then he heard her say, "I need you to watch the kids tonight. Overnight. Come over before dinner, feed them, put them to bed, get them up in the morning, feed them again, and get them to school. Can you do that?"

"Why do you need me to? Where will you be?"

"I'm allowed to have a social life, you know."

Jesus, Jericho's recently widowed stepmother had a date? An overnight date? "With who?"

"None of your business. Look, the last time I left them alone they got kidnapped and held hostage. They're scared of that happening again, but if their cop brother is there with his gun, they'll feel safe."

Kind of hard to argue with that. "They're still seeing the counselor at school?"

"They are, but she's useless. She just says it's going to be a gradual process and we need to make them feel safe. So make them feel safe, Jericho."

"When would I have to get there?"

"The sooner the better. How late are you working?"

"I don't know. Five or six, probably."

"Okay. Closer to five, if you can."

Shit. He was going to have to do this. "I don't know what they eat, or what they wear to school or any of that."

"They're not stupid. They can dress themselves. Order pizza for dinner, give them cereal for breakfast. It's not complicated."

"And you'll leave a number? I can reach you if something goes wrong?"

"Fine."

"Okay. Yeah. I'll be there a bit after five."

"Good."

And then she was gone. No *thanks*, of course. Not from Nikki.

Well, at least if Wade came by again, Jericho wouldn't be home to deal with him. To be confused by him. And maybe—

It wasn't a good thought. But after the kids were in bed, Jericho would be alone in the house of someone who was probably involved in smuggling drugs across the border. It would be a violation of trust, but he could poke around a little and see what Nikki was up to. He didn't want to bust her—didn't want to get stuck with the kids for any longer than necessary—but that didn't mean he couldn't look for anything that might incriminate someone else.

Might incriminate Wade. Because that was who she was working with, unless he'd completely misunderstood the situation. No proof of it, but a strong feeling. So he was going to snoop around in his recently widowed step-mother's house, hunting for evidence he could use to incriminate his ex-lover, a man who'd saved Jericho's life just over a month earlier?

What kind of person would do that?

What kind of cop wouldn't take advantage of any leads to shut down a drug smuggler?

Jericho pushed away from his desk impatiently and strode to the door of his office, then kept going right out of the building and onto the sidewalk. He'd stretch his legs, buy himself some lunch, and let things settle down in his mind.

It should have worked. But he was only a half block from the station when he noticed the car easing along beside him, and he rested his hand on his holster as he looked over, trying to seem casual. No one in the passenger seat. No gun pointing at him. The feds had gotten him paranoid, that was all.

He crouched down enough to see in the window. Probably someone hoping for directions, he figured, but changed his mind when he saw the man behind the wheel.

"Hey, Junior," Mike DeMonte said. "You going somewhere? You want a ride?"

"I was just going down to the diner," Jericho said. "I can walk."

Mike's expression didn't change, but there was a new tone in his voice when he said, "Nah, I can drive you. Get in."

The warnings all ran through Jericho's mind, not only the ones from other people but also messages from his own common sense. But if this was real, if the bikers were trying to make contact and Jericho turned them down, he'd be missing an opportunity. And it wasn't like he'd been poking anyone very hard, yet. He hadn't given anyone a reason to want to take him out.

So he walked over to the car and climbed in, settling so he was sitting a bit crooked and had more room to get his gun loose. Just in case.

Mike didn't say anything as they drove down the street, and Jericho didn't speak up when they cruised past the diner without even slowing down. He was going to have to wait for his lunch.

CHAPTER 8

"Where're we headed?" Jericho asked after they were well out of town, on their way up into the mountains. They hadn't left the main road, but there were no other cars in sight. At this time of year, traffic was always sparse. Not that it got much heavier any other time.

"We're just going for a drive," Mike replied casually.

Should Jericho be trying to work his cell phone loose? He could dial Kayla, let her hear whatever conversation he and Mike were having, and then she could track him using his GPS. But with what end in mind? Did he want her to burst into whatever was going on and rescue him?

No, he didn't think so. No rescue needed. He was fine, and didn't want to mess up whatever chance he might have to get some more information.

They pulled into a spot where the shoulder widened into a sort of parking area, forest sloping up beyond it, cliff falling away on the far side of the road. Broad daylight, reasonably public area. Everything was good.

Mike opened his door and climbed out, still without speaking, and Jericho followed him. "Okay, seriously, what's up? I have shit to do today, so you can either start talking or—or I guess I'll have to hitchhike back to town."

"Settle down," Mike said. He sounded amused, before saying more seriously, "Hey, can I borrow your cell? My battery's dead and I need to make a call."

It was a setup. Jericho might not be used to undercover work, but he wasn't completely witless. Still, he had no idea how to refuse without sending the whole conversation south. *The bikers have no reason to want me dead.* He fished the phone out of his pocket, keyed in the password, and handed it over.

Mike looked down at the screen. "No coverage." He tapped a few buttons, then slipped the phone into his pocket. "I'll hang on to it, and maybe I'll try the call a few miles down the road."

"What's going on, Mike? Why am I out here, and what are we doing that you don't want me to have a phone for?"

Mike sighed. "I just wanted us to have a little talk."

"Excellent. Talking sounds like a definite improvement."

"Don't get all touchy, man. This was how the last guy wanted it. We always had to meet out of town, away from spying eyes."

It was tempting to observe that picking someone up on Main Street in the middle of the day wasn't exactly keeping things on the down-low, but Jericho managed to bite that comment back in favor of asking, "The last guy?"

"Posniewski."

"Oh. Posniewski." The ex-deputy had confessed to selling department information to the bikers, but the bikers weren't supposed to *know* he'd confessed. The bastard was living it up down in Helena, sitting on his fat ass in protective custody as his lawyers worked out the details of his deal. But Mike didn't seem too worried about any of that, and Jericho needed to keep talking about the current issue. "So you're looking for a replacement? You're going to pay me for information? We need to set up what kind of intel you'd find interesting, and how much you're willing to pay."

"Slow down, now. It would be illegal for us to buy confidential information from you. And I'm not saying we bought anything from Posniewski, either. He just liked to talk to us, sometimes. Community policing, I think you'd call it. And we trusted him with some of our money, so he could make donations to the people he knew needed it most. You know, because as a police officer, he saw people having a tough time, and he wanted to help them. But you guys don't get paid shit, so he couldn't do it on his own." Mike smirked, almost comically smug with his double-talk.

"That sounds like a good system." Jericho crossed the road and peered over the barrier, down the cliff. Kay would kick his ass, but he couldn't walk away from something like this. "I'd like to be part of your system. I see a lot of people in need every day. And, yeah, like I said yesterday, it's important that locals stand together against all this out-of-state bullshit. You want to call it community policing? I'm fine with that."

Mike moved to stand beside Jericho, and they stared down the cliff together for a few moments before Mike said, "The community needs to deal with the out-of-towners, for sure. And we're expecting more trouble from them. The first three who came? Well, it was really too bad what happened there. I guess they made a mistake, and this isn't a business that accepts a lot of mistakes."

"What mistake did they make?" Jericho asked, but there was no answer, so he changed tacks. "You know where these guys are coming from? Who's sending them?" He waited to give Mike a chance to speak, then kept going. "You know what they want? They coming all this way and making all this fuss for a little weed?"

"I think maybe you misunderstood. The idea is that the information will come *from* you, not *to* you."

"How can I know what information will be useful to you if I don't know what's going on?"

Mike snorted. "Right now, we don't need any information from you. Seems like we've got a hell of a lot more than you do. What we *do* need is a show of support. We need new visitors to realize we've got law enforcement under control. We need to show outsiders you won't be a problem for us, but *will* be a problem for them. You know?"

"You want to *show* them. What exactly have you got in mind?"

Mike's smile was slow and lazy. As irritating as Wade's, with none of the added sexiness. "Be patient."

Jericho didn't have to follow that instruction for long. He heard the approaching vehicle before he saw it, a low hum that turned into a rumble as the heavy SUV pulled around a bend a hundred yards or so away. It approached slowly, so Jericho had lots of time to see Mike looking satisfied and completely unsurprised by this arrival.

"What's going on, Mike?"

"You're being useful. Keeping the peace, serving and protecting. All that wholesome cop shit."

"Could I get a few more details on that?"

But Mike didn't answer, just waited as the SUV pulled to the side of the road in front of them and the driver's door opened. The man who stepped out was younger than Jericho had expected. Well-dressed in a suit that made Jericho's beige polyester feel even itchier than usual, with his blond hair blowing just a little in the breeze. He looked like he belonged on Wall Street, not the Montana back roads.

"What the hell is this?" the new arrival growled, still close enough to the open SUV door that he could dodge back in if things went bad. "You said we'd meet alone."

"You want me to believe you haven't got someone crouched down behind the seats, hiding behind your tinted fucking windows?" Mike spat on the ground. "And you think I haven't got a couple guys in the woods with sniper rifles? Our *meeting* will be just the two of us. And the deputy is here to make sure that's how it goes down."

The newcomer barely flicked his eyes in Jericho's direction. "This isn't a good start to our relationship."

"It's a fine start. You're interested in doing business in our area, and we're interested in making it crystal fucking clear that you won't be pushing us around." Mike stopped talking for long enough to jerk his head at Jericho. "Go wait by the car."

Jericho wasn't going to hear anything useful from way over there. But he wouldn't hear anything useful if he started a fight with Mike about it, either, so he did as he was told. Mike probably loved that, getting to show off his tame under-sheriff in front of the stranger. Damn it, Jericho was someone's tool, again, and he didn't think he was getting much in return. He had no strategy, was being reactive instead of proactive, was in way over his head. Wade had been right, the smug bastard. If Jericho'd had a plan and playing a part in this little display had been part of a larger strategy, that would have been one thing. But as it was?

He couldn't even catch a glimpse of the SUV's license plate. He made sure he kept his eyes on the blond guy, memorizing enough details that he'd be able to pick him out of mug shots. But something about the way the man carried himself made it seem unlikely that there'd *be* any mug shots of him. This guy didn't move like he'd spent any time in the penal system. He was too damn smooth for that.

The two were still talking, still too faintly for Jericho to hear, so he spent some time scanning the tree line for signs of the snipers Mike had mentioned. The forest here was different than Afghanistan, sure, but the same general principles applied, and it was nice to focus on an area where he was confident. He worked out sight lines, analyzed the opportunity for cover, searched for signs of movement or the telltale glint of sunlight off a scope.

Mike and the new guy kept talking, looking over the railing down the slope like a mismatched pair of tourists admiring the view. Whatever the topic of their conversation, it didn't boil over into anything more dramatic. On the surface, they still seemed casual as they parted. No loud threats, no hurled obscenities. But there was no handshake, either, and as Mike stalked back toward his car, his expression was fixed in a snarl. "Get in," he growled at Jericho.

Well, it was either that or walk down the mountain on his own, so Jericho did as he was told. Possibly he was being too prosaic about all this and should be making some sort of a stand in the name of— the name of something. The independence of the police force, or at least the importance of not being a pussy. But he'd gotten in the car and come up the mountain because he'd wanted to get in tighter with Mike and the bikers, and there was no point ruining any progress he might have made.

So how would a weak, willing-to-be-corrupted cop respond to the current situation? "I could have used some warning on that," Jericho said as Mike peeled out and headed back to town. Jericho watched the other car in the passenger-side mirror, but still couldn't see a license plate or anything interesting. "I mean, I'm happy to help, and I hope I did. But if we're going to be working together, I need to know what's going on. You know?"

"We'll tell you what you need to know," Mike said.

"*We*? Last I heard, it was your uncle running the show with the Mountaineers. Should I be congratulating you on your upward mobility?"

"Larry's still in charge." Then Mike looked over at Jericho and said, "Technically," with the weight of a thousand bullets.

Oh, good, a power struggle in the biker gang at the same time all the rest of this shit was going down? That should lead to perfect stability. "But I follow *your* lead?" he asked, trying to sound impressed without going overboard. "Whatever's going on with these out-of-towners, you're the one handling that?"

"Yeah," Mike said. "You follow my lead." Then he glanced over in Jericho's direction. "But you don't cause any trouble with Larry. You don't challenge him, you don't disrespect him. Clear? He's still president of the club."

"Got it," Jericho said. And then, hoping he was moving things in a convincing direction, "I'm glad I was able to help with your meeting just now. But, you know, I've seen some other places I'd like to help. Not with you guys, with—like you said—with people in the community. But I'll need money to get started with that."

Mike drove quietly for a while, then said, "You need to watch yourself, Crewe. Don't get pushy."

Damn it, how would a crooked cop react to that? Why did cops go crooked in the first place, and how would that influence their decisions at times like this? Jericho almost snorted, thinking of the drama-class cliché. *What's my motivation?* He'd driven a few thousand miles away from Hollywood and *now* he was trying to turn into a damn actor?

Well, fuck it. Maybe he needed to let a little of his own personality come through. "I need to watch myself?" He twisted in his seat so he was facing Mike, who had to keep his eyes mostly on the road. "Fuck that. I'm willing to talk about a partnership, here, Mikey, something mutually beneficial. But if you're just looking for someone you can push around, someone to be your bitch? Find another sucker."

"Jesus, Crewe, cut the drama! You're as twitchy as your old man."

They were back in town, now, coming up to a yellow light at the first intersection. "Give me my phone back," Jericho demanded.

"Settle down," Mike replied. "I'll give it back when we're done."

The car had almost stopped for the now-red light. Jericho slapped the automatic transmission into park with one hand and grabbed the keys out of the ignition with the other. Then he pushed his door open and climbed out of the car, keys in his left hand, right hand free in case he needed to grab for his sidearm. It was probably stupid to escalate the situation, but he wasn't generally known for doing the smart thing.

Mike was already out of the car on the other side, staring across at Jericho, surprise fighting with anger in his expression.

"We're done *now*," Jericho told him. "Give me my fucking phone."

They were facing off against each other when Jericho caught a flash of colored lights in the corner of his eye and heard a single yelp from a police siren. Neither man broke eye contact, but Jericho could see Mike begin to reassess the situation.

"You need backup, Crewe?" Kayla asked, loud but controlled. Jericho knew she'd be standing in a position similar to his, shielded by her car door, hand near her firearm. In addition to having good timing, Kayla had good technique.

"Do I need backup?" Jericho asked Mike.

Anger won the fight on Mike's face, but the man wasn't stupid enough to take on two armed officers in broad daylight. "You need to get a fucking sense of humor," he growled.

"Mr. DeMonte's going to be reaching into his pocket to retrieve a cell phone," Jericho called in Kayla's direction, still not taking his eyes from the other man. Then in a quieter voice he added, "We might be able to work together. But no more of this picking me up on Main Street bullshit, and no more power games. You want something from me, you can leave a note in my mailbox. And you can damn well make sure I'm compensated for my time and the risk involved. Clear?"

The anger had faded from Mike's face. "Your old man was a tough son of a bitch," he said as if it were somehow relevant to the current conversation.

Jericho bit back the retort about his old man being a fucking loser. It seemed like he was doing okay in this exchange, so now he needed to keep his mouth shut and not mess it up.

After another moment, Mike reached into his pocket and pulled out the phone. He tossed it across the hood of the car, and Jericho managed to drop the keys on the hood and catch the phone with his left hand, keeping his right near his gun. But Mike made no hostile move, and Jericho stuffed the phone in his own pocket, reclaimed the keys, and tossed them across to Mike.

He stepped away from the car as Mike climbed in, sketched a jaunty salute in Kayla's direction, and then pulled away.

Jericho and Kayla watched him leave, and then she said, "You want to tell me what the hell is going on?" in a tone that made it clear *no* was not going to be an acceptable answer.

"I'll have to explain it to the feds too. Want to just hold off on the explanation until we get back and talk to them?"

"No," she said with a fierce glare. "I think I can decide whether to fire my under-sheriff without needing any input from the DEA, thank you. Once I've determined whether you're still employed by my department, then you can give your statement to the feds."

"Oh," he said, and decided it would be best not to ask her if they could go get some lunch before they talked.

CHAPTER 9

"**Y**ou said you'd be here just after five," Nikki said. She already had her keys in her hands and was heading out the door Jericho had come through. "It's almost six o'clock!"

She was in too much of a hurry to give him a full yelling at, though, and she jogged down the walkway from the house with only a few more muttered obscenities, and then Jericho turned to peek into the living room. Nicolette was sitting on the couch with the TV remote in her hand, ignoring him completely; Elijah was in the kitchen doorway looking mildly interested.

"Can I shoot your gun?" the boy asked.

Jericho had come right over from the station after dealing with hours of questions and speculation about his brief interactions with Mike DeMonte, and hadn't had time to change out of his uniform or lock up his weapon. So now, in addition to scratchy polyester hell and job tension, he also had to deal with a gun-obsessed six-year-old. "Guns aren't toys," he tried. "When you're older, I can teach you to shoot—or somebody can, at least. But you're too young."

"No, I'm not," Elijah said with quiet confidence. "We can shoot it in the backyard."

"You live in town, now. Nobody can shoot guns in the yard, and *you* can't shoot guns anywhere, not when you're so little. Give it a few years."

"Poppa let me shoot *his* guns," Elijah said.

The name was actually more surprising than the idea of Eli letting a little kid use his guns. Jericho couldn't remember a time when he'd been considered too young to shoot, and he'd been bringing home game, in or out of season, since he was ten or so. For a family without a lot of money, the forest had been better than the grocery store. But that had been a couple of decades earlier, and he hadn't had an older brother, or even an older half brother, who could have taken care of him. Elijah didn't need to be handling guns anytime soon. So maybe it was time for a redirect.

"Did you have fun with your poppa?" Jericho asked. It was the first time he'd heard the kids mention their father, and wasn't sure if it was significant. "I'm sorry he's gone. You must miss him."

Elijah's face shuttered instantly, and he headed back toward the kitchen.

"What are you making us for dinner?" Nicolette asked from her spot on the couch.

"Your mom said we should order pizza."

"We had pizza last night, and leftovers for lunch."

Thanks, Nikki. "We could get different toppings."

"We only like it with cheese and meat cookies."

"Meat cookies?"

Nicolette scowled at him like he was stupid. "Yeah. But we don't want that tonight. You can make us something."

Jericho wasn't sure he was quite ready to abandon his inquiries into the "meat cookie" idea, but supposed he had bigger worries. "We could get something else delivered. Burgers, or chicken, or whatever." The pizza place was the only restaurant that delivered, technically, but most of the others would figure out a plan if he asked nicely enough.

If he had to, he'd call the station and get one of the deputies to pick an order up for them; Kayla was still pissed at him, but she seemed to have backed down from wanting him unemployed, so he had a bit of weight to throw around. And if there was ever an occasion that justified some extra support, getting these kids fed would be it.

"You can't cook at all?" Nicolette asked.

"You want to turn off the TV and cook with me?"

She frowned. "Mom said *you* were going to make dinner."

"Yeah, well, your mom's not the boss of me."

"I'm going to tell her you said that."

Jericho had to laugh at the chill of apprehension that shivered down his spine. He'd spent the afternoon getting yelled at by one woman, and now he was worrying about getting yelled at by another one? It was a damn good thing he was gay, because apparently he had absolutely no ability to maintain an equal relationship with the females in his life.

Not that Kayla had been as out of line as Nikki was almost guaranteed to be, of course. Kayla was his boss, and in front of the feds she'd given him instructions to clear any future actions with her and avoid cowboy bullshit. He'd only made it a couple of hours before he explicitly ignored her orders. Yeah, she had the right to be pissed. Nikki, on the other hand?

"Elijah, what do you want for dinner?" he called. "We'll order in."

A blond head poked around the kitchen door. "If I eat broccoli, can I shoot your gun?"

"What? No. I don't care if you eat broccoli. I was thinking burgers or something. No shooting."

"If I tidy my room, can I shoot it?"

"I don't care if you tidy your room. No shooting."

It clearly wasn't the answer Elijah was looking for. "Maybe tomorrow?"

"Stop being stupid," Nicolette told him. "He's not going to let you because you're a stupid baby!"

"Uh, no—" Jericho started, but he was too late. Elijah had already launched himself across the room, arms flailing, screaming as he went. He had more energy than efficiency, so he wasn't doing much actual harm, and Nicolette had obviously been expecting the attack and was over on her back, kicking at her brother whenever he got too close.

"Stupid sucky baby," she singsonged.

"Fuck you, bitch," Jericho's cherubic little brother replied, and things went downhill from there.

It was hard to get between them when they were so quick and so damn low to the ground, and hard to break them up while Jericho had to be careful not to hurt either one. "Stop it," he tried, but there was no way either of them could hear him over their own shrieked obscenities.

He finally got a good grip on Elijah and lifted him straight up in the air, turning to avoid a kick from Nicolette that would have hit dangerously close to his own balls. It might have been over, except Nicolette swarmed up to the back of the couch and then took a flying leap at Jericho, landing somewhere near his shoulders where she grabbed hold of his hair and then pulled herself up to lunge at her brother.

That was when the front door slammed shut, and both kids froze. "Shit," Nicolette whispered, a good vocalization of Jericho's own mental response, and all three of them turned somewhat guiltily toward the door.

"Have I come at a bad time?" Wade asked, his expression serious enough to make it clear he was truly amused.

"Uncle Wade!" Nicolette cried, and she slithered down Jericho's body and ran for the door.

"Did you bring your gun?" Elijah asked, squirming to free himself from Jericho's grip.

Jericho let the boy go. If the battle resumed, it would be Wade's— *Uncle* Wade's—problem. But Elijah joined his sister in hugging Wade's legs as if there had never been anything but love and understanding between them.

Jericho looked up from the touching scene and found Wade's gaze on him.

"Hope it's okay that I stopped by," Wade said. "I did knock, but I guess you were a little distracted."

"Wade," Jericho said. He knew what the feds would say about this visit, knew what Kayla would say. Really, what any person with any damn common sense would say. But he was Jericho, so instead he came up with, "I'm glad you're here." And he meant it.

CHAPTER 10

Everything got easier with Wade involved. It turned out pizza for dinner two nights in a row wasn't that big of a deal, and meat cookies were slices of pepperoni. Wade hadn't brought his gun and appeared willing to follow Jericho's lead in terms of not promising future shooting opportunities, and for some reason Elijah was now willing to accept that. Pajamas were donned while pizza was being ordered, and later the kids sat on the couch and ate dinner like almost-civilized human beings.

Throughout, Jericho felt like he was in an alternate universe. It was him, and it was Wade. They weren't fighting and they weren't about to fight, as far as Jericho could tell. There didn't even seem to be all that many innuendos and hidden messages being sent, although it was possible they were there and Jericho was just too dazed to pick up on them. But he didn't think so. Most of Wade's attention was focused on the kids, listening to their tales of funny friends and cruel teachers as if the stories were actually interesting, and maybe true.

"Now, sometimes a man has to tolerate that sort of thing," Wade told Elijah as the boy chomped on a pizza crust and recounted a horrible story about unjust imprisonment at recess time. "But he can always learn from it, and find ways to turn it to his advantage. Can you think of ways you could have made this punishment work for you?"

Despite himself, Jericho was interested in hearing the answer, and Nicolette seemed pretty engaged as well.

"He could have stolen something out of someone's desk," she suggested. "If he was the only one in the room and the teacher wasn't paying attention, it would have been easy."

Wade nodded sagely. "Easy to steal, yes. But there's more to stealing than taking the item in question. You also need to be sure you aren't *caught*. And if there was no one else in the room? If the item was in someone's desk before recess, and then after recess it wasn't there, and if young Elijah was the only student in the room when the item went missing? Would he be caught?"

"Yeah, probably," Nicolette admitted.

"Also, stealing is wrong," Jericho tried. "Taking something that doesn't belong to you is—it's wrong. You wouldn't like it if somebody stole your stuff, would you?"

The other three looked at him with calm, remote pity. "I don't have anything anyone wants to steal," Elijah finally explained.

"But you might someday. And if you break the rules now, the rules might not be there to protect you when you need them." But *someday* was too far away, he realized, and *might* was too uncertain. How did he argue that people should uphold a system when that system had never done a damn thing for them? "You'd be in a lot of trouble if you got caught," he finished lamely.

"Exactly," Wade said. There was something in his expression that made Jericho want to drag him from the room and find a quiet place where it would be just the two of them. Jericho would pin Wade down, make him admit that he understood Jericho's struggle, and make him share his own. If they could be honest with each other, just them, without all the rest of the crap the world wanted to throw at them—

"So how *could* I make it work for me?" Elijah asked slowly.

And Wade kept his gaze locked on Jericho's as he said, "You could use the opportunity to get close to the authority figure. Your teacher can get you in trouble, right? But there's some judgment involved there. Sometimes she'll look the other way, or let herself be fooled. And if she likes you, she'll be more likely to see the best in you. If you can get her to trust you, you might be able to use her. Maybe she can tell you things you need to know, or you can tell *her* things so she'll act against your enemies instead of against you."

Jericho stared at Wade, and all the warm comfort he'd been enjoying froze into hard ice. So much for no innuendo or hidden meanings. What the hell was Wade saying, and why was he saying it?

Was it a warning, or a dare, or something else, something inescapably, indefinably *Wade*?

"I don't get it," Elijah said.

Wade turned his gaze back to the boy, and Jericho's eyes felt somehow heavier now that they were being ignored. "If your teacher likes you, she'll be nice to you," Wade said. "Being alone with her is a good chance to make her like you. You could offer to help her with what she's doing. Or apologize for misbehaving, and make up some explanation for why you did it. Something she'd believe."

"Like what?"

"You could always go with 'things are rough at home.' That's a good one." Wade glanced at Jericho. "Does that work for you, Under-sheriff? Does a difficult childhood excuse all misdeeds?"

Jericho surged to his feet. He had no idea where he was going, but he needed some space. "It's past eight. You guys should go to bed."

"No, not yet," Nicolette tried.

"It's time," Wade said, and the damn kids rose to their feet like obedient little robots.

"What do you need to do before bed?" Jericho asked. "Brush your teeth?"

"No, we don't have to," Elijah said.

"That's gross," Wade told him. "Go brush your teeth."

Jericho thought about trailing after them to be sure they actually followed through on the order, but it would be too disheartening to see their perfect compliance with the will of Uncle Wade. So he gathered the plates and pizza boxes and headed for the kitchen.

He was aware of Wade following after him but pretended he wasn't. Wade stood quietly, waiting, as Jericho washed the dishes and put them on the drain board, hung the dishrag on the sink, and then rearranged the soap and moisturizer on the counter.

"You about done?" Wade asked.

"What are you doing here, Wade?" Jericho had meant for his voice to sound impatient, without the plaintive note.

Wade didn't answer right away. Instead he shifted around and looked at Jericho from the side before he said, "I heard you were babysitting and thought you might need some help with the kids."

"That's all. You just wanted to be sure the kids were okay."

"I can have multiple motivations. I can want different things all at the same time."

Jericho felt the conversational ground shifting like quicksand and fought to get back to something more solid. "You're pretty good with them. You spending a lot of time around here?"

"A bit."

"Yeah." Jericho turned to look at the man head-on. "You're Uncle Wade. And you didn't get Elijah off the ash pile because you've got natural authority, you did it because you've already gotten to know him and train him. That doesn't happen fast, especially not with these kids. Is Nikki working for you, Wade? Are you dragging their *mother* into your crap?"

"Working for me? The bar blew up, remember? You were there. You think anyone's working there anymore?"

As if the bar was the only business interest Wade had. "You made your insurance claim yet?"

Wade raised an eyebrow. "The bar wasn't insured."

"Wasn't insured? So then why the hell did you—" Jericho caught himself. Did he actually want to hear the answer to that question? Did he want to know any more about Wade's nefarious dealings than he already did?

Elijah's voice came from down the hall. "Are you going to tuck us in or what?"

"Yeah, we're waiting," Nicolette called.

"Which one do you want?" Wade asked.

"Whoever I choose will just cry until you come in, anyway."

"You could take Elijah, and let him sleep with your gun. Then you'd be his favorite."

"Is that how you won the honors?"

"*My* popularity is based on my natural charm and charisma." Wade smiled sweetly. "*You* might need to use bribes."

"Go put the kids to bed," Jericho said. "You do both of them. I'll try to figure out what I'm supposed to send with them for lunch tomorrow, 'cause I'm guessing Nikki didn't put anything together."

"Yes, dear," Wade said, and disappeared down the hallway.

It *did* feel strangely domestic. Emphasis on the *strange* part. This wasn't something he'd ever wanted. A house and a family? No, not for him, and his experiences with Elijah and Nikki definitely reinforced that inclination.

But spending time with Wade? When the kids were asleep—assuming they ever actually *did* sleep without drinking human blood as a bedtime snack and then hanging upside down from their clawlike feet—it would be just Wade and Jericho. Would Wade leave right away? If he'd only come over to look after the kids, as he'd said, there'd be no reason for him to stay.

He'd already delivered his little make-people-in-authority-like-you speech, so if that had been his extra motivation for the visit, he was done. But if Jericho got lucky, Wade might stick around long enough to explain why he'd *given* the damn speech. Had he been taunting Jericho? Maybe it was part of the fun, like an added challenge. It was too easy to manipulate and use Jericho, so he'd decided to come right out and tell Jericho what he was doing. As if Jericho hadn't known all along.

Maybe it was one more customized Wade Granger mind fuck, specially designed to keep Jericho perpetually off-balance.

"You figure anything out?" Wade asked quietly from the doorway.

It took Jericho a moment to understand. "Oh. Lunch? No, not unless they want to have a bag of iceberg lettuce and some mustard."

"You and I both had worse lunches pretty often when we were their age."

"Is this the buildup to a 'difficult childhood' excuse?" Jericho shook his head. He didn't want to get into that, not when he knew Wade would use any discussion as an opportunity to tie Jericho up into knots even tighter than the current batch. "I'll pick something up for them tomorrow on the way to school."

"Store-bought lunch. Fancy."

And then they both just stood there in Nikki's kitchen, watching each other. Waiting.

"Are you out, Wade?" Jericho didn't know where the question had come from, exactly, but seeing Wade's expression, he was glad he'd asked it. It was pretty sweet to see the bastard being the uncertain one for a change.

"Out? Like out of the closet?"

"Yeah. Does the town know you're gay? Or maybe I should ask if you *are* gay. You said you had some 'friends,' but you never specified if they were male or female. So I guess the question is a bit more complex." Damn, it felt good to be in the driver's seat, at least temporarily. "How would you characterize your sexual preferences? And are these preferences common knowledge?"

"Why are you asking?"

"Why are you answering a question with a question?" Jericho shook his head. "But, for old times' sake, let me answer. I'm asking because I want to be sure I don't accidentally out you. If you're not acknowledging past indiscretions, I should make sure I keep my mouth shut about them."

Wade was closer now, although Jericho couldn't remember having seen him actually shift his feet. Shit, maybe Jericho had been the one to move.

"And that's the only reason you're thinking about this right now?" Wade raised an eyebrow, making his disbelief clear.

"What, I can only have one reason at a time? I can't have multiple motivations?"

"You can," Wade said. "You can want lots of things at the same time."

There probably wasn't any extra emphasis on *want*, but Jericho felt it anyway, and he totally lost track of the conversation. He'd been asking a question, hadn't he? Had Wade answered? "Gay," he blurted out. "We were talking about whether you're gay. Out. Did you want to confirm or deny, or do you want me to just keep blundering around, not knowing what to tell people when they ask?"

Wade's smile wasn't quite a smirk, but it was pretty damn close. "Are a significant number of people asking you about that? Is it a pressing concern for them?"

"They aren't always *direct* questions," Jericho admitted. Wade was even closer now, close enough that Jericho's brain, not a smoothly running machine to begin with, had stalled almost completely.

"But you feel like you should have an answer," Wade said calmly. It was always dangerous when Wade seemed helpful and understanding. Hell, it was always dangerous when he seemed to be *anything*.

"I guess so," Jericho said. "Yeah, I should have an answer." Wade was right there in front of him, and his gray eyes were warm, his lips smiling, his body balanced and ready, alert without being tense.

"Okay," Wade agreed slowly. "Next time someone asks you? You can tell them this." Then his hand was somehow on the back of Jericho's neck, confident and warm, totally natural, as if this was something they did whenever they felt like it. He pulled, only a little, and Jericho's body responded without any conscious direction.

They were close to the same height, so there was no stretching, no bending. It was a meeting in the middle, an easy compromise they never seemed to be able to find in any real-world situation. Wade's lips were warm and the kiss was almost sweet. There were no demands, no challenges, and no damned confusion. Just Wade, and just Jericho.

Jericho's hand gripped Wade's waist and dragged him in more tightly. This was a terrible idea for so many different reasons, but none of them mattered, not in comparison to the perfection of the kiss.

They staggered a little, but neither of them was willing to pull away far enough to regain their balance. The kitchen wasn't large, and they stumbled into the wall pretty quickly, Wade's back against it while Jericho pressed in against him. Impossible, infuriating, inescapable Wade, and Jericho had him now, had him controlled and contained. The kiss deepened, both of them exploring and reclaiming territory that they'd both once known so well.

One of Wade's hands tangled in Jericho's hair, the other found his ass and dragged him in. So many years apart, and still this all just *worked*.

They both jumped when Jericho's cell phone rang, vibrating between his ass and Wade's hand. "Leave it," Wade ordered, and he leaned forward, chasing Jericho's mouth.

"That's Kay's ring." Jericho felt like he was swimming through a fog, like he was just waking up and wasn't yet sure what was real and what was imagined. "She doesn't call unless she needs me."

And somehow he found the strength to pull himself away. Wade stood there against the wall, lips swollen and slick with their shared spit, eyes darker and deeper than they'd ever been before, and Jericho still managed to fumble his phone out and answer it.

"What's up?" he asked, sounding only a little breathless.

"We need you at the station," Kayla said. "We've got an explosion at the Mountaineer headquarters, and the Canadian cops called to let us know they tracked a shipment to the border and saw it go across. We haven't picked anyone up yet on our side, but the feds are out hunting, and they want local support. Things are going down tonight, Jericho. I need you here."

"I'm babysitting." He'd told her that earlier, but couldn't be surprised if it had slipped her mind. "I'd like to come in, but I can't leave the kids alone."

"Megan Stewart is on her way; she's Garron's niece, and she's great with kids. You leave them with her and get in here, okay?"

Shit. Nikki would kill him, of course, but— He froze, and stared at Wade, who was looking back at him. Waiting. Watching as Jericho put the pieces together.

"I'll be in as soon as I can," he said into the phone, and ended the call.

Wade was still waiting. He didn't appear apprehensive, exactly. Nothing so human. But he seemed expectant.

"Why'd you really come by here tonight?" Jericho asked, trying to keep his voice level.

Wade's smile was a horrible mix of sweetness, regret, and ironic detachment. "I can have multiple motivations, Jay."

The knock at the front door was the only thing that kept Jericho from punching the duplicitous bastard in the face.

CHAPTER 11

The sheriff's office was almost empty when Jericho arrived, but Kayla was there, pacing restlessly. "They want my officers, but not my leadership," she told him as he walked in the door. "Just like the last time they were here. I thought we were past that, but I guess they changed their minds."

There was no need to clarify who *they* were. Damn feds. "They pushed you right out? Seriously? Out of the bikers *and* the smuggling?"

"They appreciate my continued cooperation," she said bleakly.

"Shit. Sorry. Is there anything we *can* do, without stepping on their toes?"

"This is a bit of a turnaround." She gave a bitter laugh. "They're hoping you're going to be able to help them out with the bikers—if this was a deliberate attack, they think the bikers might contact you to help them with reprisals." She looked at him, waited a moment, then added, "So now you're in, and I'm out. And suddenly you're worrying about stepping on their toes."

"You give me the word and I will stomp with both feet, Kay, I promise. I was just thinking about you. You've been damn good to them, and put up with all their crap, and now they're trying to push you out? Why?"

"They're not being completely clear. Well, they're not being clear at all, in terms of reasons, but they're not shy about telling me to butt out."

"When did this happen? They were okay with you until—they were okay with you earlier today, weren't they?"

"I'm not sure. They didn't freeze me right out until tonight, but I think maybe they've been cooling on me for a while."

"Because of me?"

"The world doesn't revolve around you, Jay. They could have a whole separate set of issues they'll share when they're good and ready." She was quiet for a moment, then shook her head. "Fuck them. This is my town, and I know all the players. They don't want me in the field? I can do my job from in here. I want us to talk this through. You and me, we can figure things out." She didn't wait for an answer. "The bikers got firebombed tonight. Is it safe to assume it was the Chicago guys, as part of this turf war?"

Jericho sighed. His life would be a lot easier if that was a safe assumption. "We've had another firebombing in town recently. Be a bit coincidental if they weren't connected. And Wade says there was no insurance on his bar. Which makes it unlikely that he torched the place himself. It wasn't insurance fraud; it was someone going after him."

"Wade said the place wasn't insured? You didn't mention it when we talked about all this with the feds." Her look wasn't suspicious, but cautious.

"He said it tonight. He showed up at Nikki's house when I was babysitting."

She stared at him, and he raised his hands defensively. "I didn't ask him to come over, and I didn't know he was going to be there." *I didn't ask him to stick his tongue down my throat, and I didn't know how perfect it would be when he did.* "It's weird, obviously, but if he was telling the truth, that's relevant information."

"Is he trying for some sort of 'poisoned fruit' approach for a future trial?" she mused. "Any evidence he gives to you without Miranda warnings will be inadmissible, and so will anything we learn based on what he said."

"For Miranda to apply, I'd have to be questioning him as part of my duties as a law enforcement officer. Right? But in this case I was babysitting and he showed up at the door. I was a long way from being on the job. So, I don't know what he's up to, but I don't think Miranda is a part of it." He gave her enough time to object to that, then continued. "Seems like somebody burned his place down to teach him a lesson or to knock him back a little."

"We haven't gotten a report from the Mountaineers' crime scene yet," she said. "No way to tell if it's the same MO as Kelly's."

"Be interesting to see that." If similar techniques were used, it would suggest that the same people were responsible for both explosions, which would suggest the Chicago gang had gone after Wade first, then the bikers. If the method was different, it might mean Wade had taken his revenge on the bikers for burning his place. "Anybody hurt or killed?"

"A few injuries so far, but nothing too serious. Apparently the bikers were having a bonfire out in the back of the property, so the building was empty. Or that's what we're hoping—the fire crews are still working through the wreckage."

"No one injured at Wade's, either." He wasn't sure if that was significant or not. Three dead bodies from Chicago suggested that at least one side of this war wasn't too worried about minimizing casualties.

But Kayla's mind was following a different track. "Wade just happened to be with you when this all went down," she said, her gaze level on Jericho. "So he's got a damn reliable alibi."

"Yeah," he admitted. "That thought occurred to me as well." And it had made him want to punch Wade in the face, but he didn't bother sharing that detail. "Even if he was establishing an alibi, though, it might not be about the explosion. You mentioned that the Canadian cops tracked a shipment to the border. Do we know who picked it up on our side?"

"The tip came too late; the Canadians got some long-distance photos, but not enough for a positive ID. And by the time our guys got there, whoever it was had disappeared into the forest."

Of course they had. The border was long and porous, practically impossible to enforce. "We know who it wasn't, though," he said. "At least who wasn't there in person."

"Wasn't Wade." She shook her head in disgust. "So whether he's covering his ass for the shipment or the explosion or both, he's in good shape." She looked down at the stack of papers she was carrying, then back up at Jericho. "The bastard could have established an alibi so many different ways. He could have gone out for dinner and been seen by the public, he could have filled up on gas at a station with a time-stamped camera. But he had to use you. It's like he's taunting us. He's playing a fucking game."

Pointless to argue. That was exactly what Wade was doing. "Nikki was planning to be out all night." He felt like a traitor for sharing this information, but he'd be even more of a traitor if he didn't. "She made it sound like a date, but when she left the house she wasn't dressed up at all. I think maybe she's working with Wade. So it might have been her who picked up the imports tonight. Might have been bikers, might have been someone from the Chicago crew, might have been someone else entirely. But, yeah. It might have been Nikki."

She was quiet for a moment. "Why do you think she's working for Wade?"

He told her about seeing Nikki on the bicycle on his trip back from the drop house. "I didn't mention it because it's so far from proof of anything. We were almost to town by the time I saw her—the timing might have been right, with me having to wait around for a while before I left the scene, and her having to pack up the place and ride her bike down the mountain. But all I *know* is that she was out for a bike ride in the same general area as the drop house the day I encountered someone there. It wasn't enough to mean anything."

"But you still think she's working for him."

"Just a feeling. Not anything concrete."

"Jesus Christ, Jay. The feds aren't wrong; you're too damn close to the players in all this. It's not your fault, but it's reality. A case this big is going to be complicated by nature of its size. If we've got an investigating officer with close ties to *two* primary suspects, it's going to get a hell of a lot messier."

"It's only Wade that's for sure involved," he tried. "I'm just guessing about Nikki. I could be wrong." And then, because he was a little tired of being on the defensive all the time, "What are the feds worried about with you? I know they found out about your illegal tracking, but that's an overenthusiasm problem, not corruption. Right? And they already knew about that when they came back, and they were still letting you in. So what's changed?"

"I have no fucking idea. Everything was fine—well, strained, but functioning—and then it just wasn't. Feels like the trouble's coming from the FBI more than the DEA, to me, but I could be wrong about that." She shrugged. "It doesn't matter all that much. Whatever the problem is, I'm out. We both are."

"Maybe not. Like you said, the bikers want to use me. If the feds want that connection, they'll have to let me in."

"The bikers might not want anything to do with you, not after your little show of backbone yesterday afternoon."

"Maybe they won't," he admitted. "But they didn't pick me at random—they want me *because* of all that shit the feds don't like. So I wouldn't be easy to replace. If the bikers stay in touch, the feds will need me."

"Hell, maybe I should point out that I used to hang around with Wade too, and see what contacts I can make."

"Nah." He grinned at her. "You're Kay the Incorruptible. Anyone who knows you knows that."

"And you're Jericho the . . .?"

"Jericho the Absent, I guess. The town knows who I used to be, and that means they think they know who I am. But I've been away a long time, and I've changed. That's what they're missing."

"And Wade?" she asked softly. "Is he still seeing you as old Jericho, or does he see the changes?"

Jericho shrugged. There was nothing to say, no way to explain that when it came to Wade, old Jericho and new Jericho seemed to be on exactly the same self-destructive page. "We've got working theories," he said instead, "but no proof. Nothing to impress the feds. We need to see the report on the firebombing so we can see if it matches Kelly's. You know anyone at the fire marshal's office? If the feds are being assholes, we might need to get the report ourselves."

"I can make a call," Kayla agreed. "Shouldn't be a problem."

"I don't know if there's much else we can do on the border crossing," Jericho said, "and, honestly, I don't care. I mean, that *is* a federal issue, and it's not one that anyone in town—any of the people who pay our salaries—really cares about all that much."

"You're okay with your stepmother being a drug runner?"

He sighed. "I'm not saying it's ideal."

She seemed like she might have more to say on the topic, but his phone rang and he looked down at the screen, then back up at her. "Feds," he said. She nodded, and he lifted the phone to his ear. "Crewe."

"We're bringing some members of the Mountaineers in to the station for questioning," Hockley's too-familiar voice told him. "We want you there to be good cop. Crooked cop. Whatever. We may not use you, but we want you on call. Be at the station in fifteen minutes."

"Is that an order? Because I take orders from the sheriff, not from you. Why don't you give her a ring and see if she's interested in loaning me out?"

"I'm sure the sheriff will be happy to cooperate."

"Great. So as soon as I hear from her, I'll come in." He ended the call without waiting for a reply.

Kay's gaze was level. "Garron says you're a pain in the ass, but you're *our* pain in the ass." When he shrugged she said, "I think I'm good with that."

Her phone rang then, and she lifted it to her ear with a sweet smile. "Special Agent Hockley? What can I do for you this evening?"

CHAPTER 12

Jericho spent most of the night hanging around, waiting to be called on. He built up a pretty good sense of resentment against the feds and their high-handed bullshit, so when he finally *was* sent in to drop off some paperwork for Hockley, he didn't have to rely on his acting skills to glower at the asshole. Five hours of sitting around in the middle of the damn night, and the bastard was using him as an errand boy?

It was Mike DeMonte in the chair across the table from Hockley, looking about as pissed off as Jericho felt, but there was no opportunity to exchange words or use their fledgling relationship to extract any information, so the whole thing seemed like a waste of time.

When the last of the interviews were finished around seven in the morning, Hockley called a meeting in the conference room that had been Jericho's extended office before the feds had shown up. Jericho and Kay were generously permitted to attend.

There wasn't too much news to share, since the bikers had uniformly denied any knowledge of recent events and there were no results back from the crime lab yet, but Hockley managed to drag we-don't-know-anything-yet into a half-hour presentation.

"This is a developing situation," he said as his speech ran down. "Thus far we've been reactive rather than proactive, but we're hoping for an opportunity to change that. We're investigating the crimes that have been committed, but we're also watching the bigger picture, looking to charge and convict perps to ensure there will be no *future* crimes. We need to be patient, but also ready to act when we have a chance."

"How long were they in town last time?" Jericho muttered to Kay. "They didn't make a single arrest, right?"

She shushed him, but her lips quirked into a little grin as she did it. Kayla respected authority, but she never would have hung out with Jericho and Wade if she didn't sometimes question it too. Especially when it was in her damn headquarters, trying to take over.

"So, we've got some fresh assignments," Hockley said, and then he looked back at Jericho and Kayla. "As I was reminded last night, members of the sheriff's department aren't actually mine to order around, so I think we're at the end of the information we need to share." His gaze was pointed. The locals were dismissed.

"You be sure to let us know if you learn, well, anything," Jericho said, his tone making it clear he wasn't optimistic about the chances of that happening.

"Or if you need any help," Kayla added. "You know, with the tricky stuff."

"Thank you for the kind offer," Hockley said. And then he waited as Kayla and Jericho left the room.

"That was a waste of a night," Jericho said as they stood outside the closed conference room door. "But at least I wasn't attacked by savage children. I should go make sure they get to school, and then I think I'll catch some sleep, unless you have something you want me to be doing?"

"Come with me for a second," she directed, and led the way to her office. She sat behind the desk, clicked a few items on her computer, then gestured for him to join her so he could see the screen.

He did as he was told, and let out a low whistle. "Advance copy of the fire marshal's report? Damn, Kay, that was fast."

"He texted me while we were in the meeting. Stresses that it's still *very* preliminary, but says all signs point to the same accelerant and technique being used at Kelly's and the Mountaineers' club house."

"So the Chicago gang hit Wade first, then the bikers?"

"Seems likely." She peered up at him. "Strange order—you'd think they'd go after the bikers first, then worry about Wade. I mean, he's involved in every damn thing, but he's more or less a solo operator. Hirelings as needed, but no standing army like the bikers have."

"Maybe they were warming up with an easier target," Jericho mused. "Or maybe they were trying to negotiate with the bikers and the talks went bad. Whatever that meeting I saw yesterday was about, I wouldn't say either party walked away happy."

"They could have killed a lot more bikers if their timing had been different. If they're taking revenge for three dead soldiers, you'd think they'd have wanted some body bags involved."

"Maybe it was deliberate—like a warning. Or maybe it was just a coincidence that the place was empty—good luck for the bikers, bad luck for Chicago."

"Too many damn maybe's," she growled, and pinched the bridge of her nose. Then she took a deep breath and squared her shoulders. "Okay. Go take care of the demon-spawn. Hopefully they haven't killed and eaten poor Megan."

"If they did, you're the one who has to tell Garron," he said.

He was downstairs and almost to the front door when someone called "Crewe!" from behind him. Jericho turned to see Hockley trotting down the stairs. "Where are you heading?"

"Bed." Jericho didn't mention the stop he was planning to make at Nikki's house, because it was none of this guy's damn business.

"Nice work in front of DeMonte." Hockley smiled. It looked creepy and wrong.

"You mean when I acted like I was sick of your shit?" Jericho shrugged. "I'm not actually a good actor."

Hockley's weird-ass smile didn't budge.

"Jesus, what are you up to now?" Jericho was too tired for any of this. "Whatever it is, you should go through Kay. She's my boss."

"And your friend," Hockley said. "You're loyal to her. That's nice to see."

"What, are you going to give me the 'I hope that loyalty isn't misplaced' speech? Because you can save it. I trust Kay way, way the hell more than I trust you, which isn't saying much since I don't trust you at all. But I do trust her, and my loyalty is placed exactly where it should be."

"I agree." Hockley's smile became almost natural. "Not that you shouldn't trust me, but I absolutely agree you should trust her. Be loyal to her. And, to be honest, I think it's important that you be her friend too." He paused, waiting for a response Jericho was completely incapable of giving.

What the hell is he up to?

"Can I buy you breakfast?" Hockley seemed . . . genuine?

Jericho finally found his power of speech. "Are you coming on to me, Special Agent Hockley?"

"Simon," Hockley said. "My name's Simon. And, no, I'm not coming on to you. But I would like to talk to you about something not strictly related to the current business. Something I'd like to discuss in a private setting, if that's okay."

"Yeah, that still sounds like you're coming on to me."

"This is serious, Jer— May I call you Jericho?"

"And *still* it feels like a come-on. So, no 'Jericho.' No 'Jay,' and no 'Sweetie Pie.' Seriously, what's going on?"

"It's about Kayla, Mr. Crewe. I'm worried about her, and I'd like you to help me look out for her. Now, can we meet somewhere that isn't in her building?"

What the hell? Hockley was trying to be an ally? A friend? Damn it, life would be easier if Jericho could just smart-ass his way out of this situation, whatever the hell it was. But Hockley was a fed, and the feds were freezing Kayla out of their investigation for an unknown reason. Regardless of Hockley's motivations, if he was willing to talk, Jericho was definitely going to listen. "We can have breakfast. But we have to make a stop, first."

It was comforting to see Nicolette and Elijah treat Hockley with even more disdain than they showed for Jericho. "That's not a real gun," Elijah confided to Jericho as they walked down the cracked asphalt of the house's driveway. He was scoffing at Hockley's hip.

"It's real," Jericho corrected firmly. "Assume all guns are real, and all guns are dangerous if you're not careful. Understand?"

"How do we know it's real? Will he shoot it?"

"Only if I have to," Hockley interrupted, but Elijah acted as if he hadn't heard a word. Damn, the kid was only six years old and he was already better at giving attitude than Jericho was.

"I'll make you a deal," Jericho said, and he crouched down next to Elijah. "I want you to think of something else you like. Something *other* than guns. And no tanks, or fighter jets or whatever. I want you to think of something that isn't designed to kill anybody. And whatever that second-most-favorite thing is? You tell me what it is, and I will work hard to get you a chance to play with it, or work with it, or whatever. But only if you stop asking me about guns all the time."

Elijah squinted at him and opened his mouth, but Jericho raised a hand. "Don't answer yet. You need to think about it. You can tell me the next time you see me, okay?"

"When's that going to be?"

"I don't know. But your mom has my phone number. If you think of a good idea and you don't see me for a while, you can give me a call and let me know. Okay?"

"Why does *he* get that?" Nicolette demanded. They were at the cruiser now, and Jericho tried not to think about how he might be establishing patterns for their futures as he helped them into the backseat. "What about me?"

Yup, Jericho should have seen that coming. "Okay, you can think of *your* most favorite thing too. Not guns or anything illegal, and we'll have the same deal."

He checked their seat belts and then shut the door, and looked over the roof of the car to see Hockley smirking at him. "You're going to have a lot of fun at the Disney Princesses show."

"Are you kidding? Nicolette? She'd probably rather go to some death metal concert."

Hockley's smirk turned into a rueful grin, and Jericho almost grinned back before he caught himself. "We need to stop at the grocery store to buy them lunch. If you think you're safe, you can stay in the car with them while I go in."

"This is a car designed to transport dangerous felons," Hockley said dryly.

"These two could slither through the bars. But like I said, if you feel safe, it'd be quicker for me to go in on my own."

"We'll be fine," Hockley assured him, and Jericho didn't argue. He did keep it quick at the grocery store, and made it to the car and then to the school without any serious trauma.

"Your mom's back on for after school," he told the kids, trying not to wonder where she'd spent the night. "But the school has my number. If she doesn't make it, ask them to give me a call."

The kids scooted out of the squad car, and Nicolette made a big show of sneering in Hockley's direction, and then they ran to the playground to find their friends.

"Were you like that at their age?" Hockley asked.

"I might have been," Jericho admitted. "But that's not what we're supposed to be talking about. What's going on with Kay?"

"You want to do this in the parking lot of an elementary school?"

"And, again, it sounds like you're coming on to me. Is there some reason we can't have a conversation in this parking lot?"

"Because I'm hungry," Hockley retorted. "I've been up all damn night, I missed dinner, I haven't had breakfast, and I'm going to go back to the damn station after this and the only stuff they'll have to eat is damn donuts and muffins. I want *breakfast*. Is that okay with you?"

Jericho carefully put the car into gear. "You get kinda grumpy when you're hungry, Simon."

Hockley snorted, then checked his watch. "We're not going to get much privacy at the diner, not at this time of day. I know I'm opening myself up to more comments about coming on to you, but I've got a sort-of dining area in my motel room, and they do room service. You okay with that?"

"You're taking the fun out of my innuendo game."

"Sorry. I guess I'm not that good at games."

Jericho raised an eyebrow. "Seems like all you do is play games. It's a shame if you haven't gotten better at them."

"I've been trying to have an honest conversation with you for the last hour, Mr. Crewe, and you've done nothing but resist. Now you're accusing *me* of playing games?"

"You *say* it's an honest conversation. But am I just supposed to believe that's true? Not move number eighty-seven in whatever chess match you've got set up?"

"Ah, poor Jericho Crewe. The only straight shooter, the only simple, honest man in a world full of deception and trickery. Is that how you see yourself? Just an old-fashioned cowboy, trying to find his white hat in a sea of black and gray."

"I'm a little tired of people calling me a cowboy," Jericho mused. "Otherwise, though, that was very poetic. Lovely, really." He decided not to mention, or even think about, Wade's claims that Jericho saw things in black and white. Assuming Wade was correct, did it strengthen or weaken whatever the hell Hockley was getting at? "Shit. I'm too tired for this. Let's go to your room and get some breakfast and then I can go to bed."

Jericho put the car in drive and started for the motel. He had no idea what Hockley had to say or why he didn't want Kayla to hear it. But Jericho could certainly listen. He could listen carefully, and maybe even take notes so he'd be sure he didn't miss anything when he told Kayla the whole story.

CHAPTER 13

"**T**he FBI is going after Sheriff Morgan," Hockley said. He'd just set the phone down after ordering from room service, and made his announcement as if it were simply another detail of his day. But Jericho half stood, ready to storm out or fight or . . . something. Hockley quickly raised a hand. "*Retired* Sheriff Morgan. I wouldn't be talking to you if they were suspicious of the current sheriff."

Jericho stared at the man. "Going after him for what? He's been retired for over a year now, hasn't he?"

"Comfortably retired," Hockley agreed. "And still earning some kickbacks from passing information along to various sources."

"Information he gets from— He's not involved in active policing anymore." Jericho wasn't going to mention the surveillance system he'd seen in Morgan's basement. "You're thinking he's getting intel from Kayla?" Jericho didn't want to hear the answer to that question, but made himself watch as Hockley nodded.

"It appears so."

"She wouldn't be part of anything corrupt. Not knowingly. Maybe she talks cases over with him, or something like that. That's normal—he's the ex-sheriff *and* her dad. It would make sense for her to bounce ideas off him and get his input, but there's no way she's passing information on purpose. No way."

"I agree," Hockley said calmly. "That's why I wanted to talk to you about it. If this were a straightforward case of corruption, you wouldn't be involved. And I should stress that technically, according to the FBI, you *aren't* involved. I got an off-the-record okay to talk to you about it, but I'm only on the periphery of this myself. I'm DEA, not FBI, and they're only letting me in because this might be part of the larger case."

"You think Morgan is selling intel to the bikers or the Chicago crew?"

"Or Wade Granger," Hockley said, busying himself with the motel room's coffeemaker, clearly pretending he wasn't waiting for a reaction to that name.

"That's who you're thinking? I mean, what evidence have you got? Are you sure on this, or are you all just looking for local law enforcement to blame so you can direct attention away from your own crooked guys?"

"You seem fairly protective of Mr. Morgan," Hockley said mildly. "It was my impression that you and he didn't get along too well?"

"I'm protective of Kayla. Not because she can't take care of herself, but because something like this, even if she's not *directly* involved, could ruin her career. And because it would tear her apart if this turned out to be true. Morgan's a pain in the ass, but he's—" *He's our pain in the ass.* Was Jericho ready to say that? No, not for a crooked cop. Not for a man who'd use his daughter this way. "He's her dad. She cares about him." He thought for a moment. "And he cares about her. He's crazy about her, totally overprotective. He wouldn't put her at risk like this, not just for money."

Hockley nodded, at least giving the impression that he was considering what Jericho was saying. "What about pride?" he asked. "Or wanting to feel like he's still part of things?"

"You think a lifelong lawman would want to be part of things by selling information to the wrong side?"

"We have strong reason to believe that he was bent while he was on the job. So continuing to be bent after he retires wouldn't be that much of a departure, really."

There was a knock at the door then, and Jericho was glad of the chance to take a break from the conversation as Hockley accepted various plates from the server and arranged them on the table.

When the woman was gone and Jericho and Hockley sat down, they ate in silence for a few bites. Then Jericho said, "So what do you want from me? Why do you want me involved? As I recall, you don't have a whole lot of trust in *my* ethical purity, so why the hell are you bringing me in on this? Just trying to make everything a tiny bit more complicated?"

Hockley finished his bite of toast without hurrying. "You've been searching for ways to prove I'm dirty; I've been doing the same for you. Neither one of us has found anything, and I'm too confident in my own investigation abilities to believe I've missed incriminating evidence. I have concerns about your personal relationships, but that's all. I need an ally, and you're it."

Jericho needed to find a job where things were simpler. "So let's say you trust me. Why do you need me, when you've got all the resources of the mighty federal law enforcement agencies at your disposal?"

"Because the federal law enforcement agencies don't give a damn about Kayla Morgan, and they will pursue their suspect regardless of the impact their investigation has on her life."

"And you won't?"

"I care about justice. I won't tolerate a dirty cop, or a dirty ex-cop who continues to break the law. If Kayla Morgan has to go down in order to stop Donald Morgan, then Kayla Morgan has to go down. But if she doesn't have to? If I can find a way to avoid that, I want to. She's a good cop, and it wouldn't serve justice for her to be punished for someone else's crime."

"I don't remember you being quite this compassionate when we were trying to find the assholes who took Nikki's kids. Seemed like you were more concerned about the case then, not so much about the kids."

"That situation was—" Hockley frowned. "I'm not proud of how I reacted in that situation. I know you have no reason to believe me, but it was a turning point for me. I believe in my job, and I will do it to the best of my ability. But in that situation, I believe I allowed my interest in justice to overwhelm my sense of compassion. It shouldn't have happened. And whether you believe me or not, working with Kayla Morgan has been important in letting me realize that. I admire the way she balances her priorities and responsibilities." Another pause. "I admire her for a great many reasons. And I don't want to see her hurt by something beyond her control."

The bastard seemed completely sincere. Jericho took a mouthful of eggs. Was this another game, another one of Hockley's manipulations? It was entirely possible. But Jericho couldn't just walk away, not if there was a chance that he could help Kayla out. "Okay," he finally said. "I agree, in principle. What are you thinking about in concrete terms?"

Hockley shrugged. "Nothing much, yet. The FBI are still building their case and recent events have distracted them a bit, so they're putting the Morgan file on the back burner, for now. But it's likely that they'll be using the current sheriff to leak information they want leaked. And hard as it is, I think you and I need to let that happen. If the bikers and the Chicago crew are at war, it could spill over and impact a lot of innocents, and we need to do everything we can to stop that, even if it hurts an innocent."

"Have you thought about just telling her what you're doing?" Jericho asked. It was a sincere question, not a sarcastic one, and Hockley seemed to take it as intended.

"I've thought about it extensively. But I just— Partly, I don't want to put her in that position. I don't want her to have to choose between doing her job and protecting her father."

"Understandable, but too bad. Kayla's a grown-ass woman. If you were in that position, you'd want to know, wouldn't you? You'd want to make that choice yourself, not have some well-meaning stranger make it for you?" Hockley didn't answer right away, so Jericho continued. "If we're protecting Kayla—if that's our number-one priority—then we treat her like an adult and we tell her what's going on, and we follow her lead."

Hockley nodded reluctantly. "I hear what you're saying. So, okay, protecting Kayla is not my number-one priority. Protecting public safety is number one. Enforcing the law is number two. Protecting Kayla? I suppose it's at number three."

"So that's why you can't tell her what's going on." Jericho sighed. "I'm not saying your priorities are wrong. I just want us to be on the same page with all this. I want us to both have the same understanding."

"And what are your priorities, Under-sheriff?"

"Same number one as you, I guess. Kayla losing her job isn't as bad as someone else losing their life. Number two? That gets a bit hazier, maybe. I mean, I believe in the law. But I believe in it because I think it's the best way to make things better for people. If a situation comes up where it's *not* the best tactic? That makes everything more complicated."

"You're on a slippery slope with that approach."

"Life is a slippery damn slope. But you show me a cop who says he's never bent the law a little, never looked the other way or let someone off with a warning when there technically should have been a charge? I'll say that cop is either a liar or an asshole." Jericho took a bite of his eggs, then added, "Possibly both. Because who but an asshole would lie about something like that?"

Hockley didn't appear insulted, which was kind of nice. Jericho wouldn't go so far as to say he was starting to *like* the guy, but Hockley at least seemed—well, he seemed like maybe he was a decent human being, underneath all the pompous fed bullshit. And if he really was looking out for Kayla, then Jericho wanted him on his side. It was a big *if*, though. Still, for the time being, Jericho would give the fed the benefit of the doubt.

And Hockley was giving Jericho the same benefit, based on his cautious nod of agreement.

"So, we both agree that protecting the public is number one." Jericho wasn't much good at making peace and finding compromises, but for Kayla's sake he'd try. "For number two and three, though? I could go tell Kayla about this right now. She'd know to cover her ass, and I don't think anyone would get hurt if I did that. If the FBI has proof that he was crooked when he was sheriff, let them use that to bust him. Or if they can't bust him, who the hell cares, as long as Kayla shuts down the information pipeline? He wouldn't have any other sources of information, would he? Or, hell, we could let him know you guys have your eyes on him and he'll stop doing whatever he's doing."

Hockley nodded slowly. "I admit, that was what I was tempted to do. There are two problems with that plan, though. The first one is, we can't turn a blind eye to corrupt policing. We don't simply need to stop it, we need to make an example of those involved. We need to make sure everyone out there knows what happens to crooked cops, so they don't get tempted to go down the same path."

Jericho shrugged. It was hard to argue with. "What's the second problem?"

"It's not a problem so much as an opportunity. Because if we know he's leaking information, but he doesn't know we know? Then we can use him. If we want to leak information—false or true—we know how to do it. That's why I let you and Kayla sit in on the first part of the briefing this morning, because I *want* her to pass that information along to her father. I *want* the perps in this case to think we don't have much to go on. And then for the part where we talked actual strategy, I excluded her."

"You kicked her out of a meeting being held in her own damn building," Jericho corrected. "You want to preserve public safety, you need to think about the effect shit like that is going to have. If she doesn't have people's respect, she can't do her job properly, and if she can't do her job, people could get hurt."

"So what do you suggest, Mr. Crewe?"

He sighed. "Okay. Fuck it. 'Jericho' is fine. And I don't really know what we should be doing. You need to find a way to deal with her more respectfully, but I'm not sure exactly how you can do that when you have to control what information she has access to. I see what you're saying . . . I just hate it that this is happening."

"I understand." Hockley sounded like he did. "And I realize I've sprung this on you fairly suddenly, and I haven't had the best working relationship. But all the same, I need to know I can count on you."

"To do what?"

"A few things. One, to pay attention to what Kayla knows, or thinks she knows. Because we have to assume anything she knows may be passed along to her father, which means it may be passed along to others. She's persistent, and she's not going to stop having theories or investigating them just because we're trying to push her out. And whatever those theories are, she'll share them with you." He was watching Jericho closely, but Jericho was pretty sure he was too conflicted to be showing a coherent response.

"She shares theories with me—and you want me to share them with you?" Jericho asked, his voice quiet.

"Yes." Hockley had the courtesy to not add any gloss to the confirmation.

Jericho wished he was somewhere else. Just about anywhere else, really. But he wasn't, so he thought for a moment, then nodded. "Yeah. Okay. I'll probably *tell* her I'm telling you. But I'll do it."

"Good."

"What's two?"

"Two is more nebulous, but possibly more important."

"I'm going to need details on that."

"I need you to be ready to move. And I need you to trust me, so if I *tell you* it's time to move, you do it."

"Move how?"

"I don't know yet. I may not know until the moment occurs."

"This seems like a pretty good deal, for you. I'm your spy and your servant, and you just use me as you see fit?"

"That's where the trust comes in." Hockley set down his fork. "I'm not sure what I can do to persuade you to trust me. Putting myself in your shoes, I can't imagine what I'd need to hear in order for that to happen. But it's important that it does."

"We could try by making the deal reciprocal," Jericho suggested mildly. "You want me to share intel with you and be prepared to act on your instructions when needed? How about you agree to do the same for me?"

It was interesting to watch the fed wrestle with the idea. "There are confidentiality rules I am not able to break," he finally said. "And I can't ignore the chain of command. I can't take action just because you tell me to."

"Huh." Jericho stood up and dropped his napkin on his chair. "I guess that settles it, then."

"So you're refusing to help? I'm offering you a way to minimize the impact this situation has on your friend, and you're walking away?"

"I'm aware of the situation. I'll keep an eye on things. If there's something I think you *should* know, I'll tell you about it. And if you want me to do something, you can tell me what it is, and I'll decided whether or not to do it. That's as good as you're going to get, I think. Other than that? I work for Sherriff Kayla Morgan. Not for you."

"What I've told you here today is part of a federal investigation. If you share any of this information with Kayla Morgan, you'll be interfering with that investigation. I don't need to remind you of the consequences of such an action. Not only for you and your career, but also for Kayla. If *she* knows and tells her father, she's implicating herself in police corruption. And if she doesn't tell him? If she knows he's under investigation and she doesn't tell him about it? Well, that'd be a hell of a thing for her to have to live with, wouldn't it?"

"I won't tell her," Jericho said slowly. He needed some time to think it all through, but Hockley was probably right, even though it felt wrong. It was better for Kayla to not know about her father, for as long as that ignorance could be maintained. "I'll do what I can, what makes sense, with the rest of it. But in terms of trusting you?" Jericho squinted at him. "I don't think you're a dirty cop. But I don't know you well enough to trust your judgment, and I've seen too many of your tricks to trust your methods. So . . . yeah. Let's play it by ear."

Hockley nodded. "Okay. If that's the best I'm going to get, I guess I'll take it."

"Don't have much choice," Jericho agreed. "Do you need a ride back to the station?"

"No. My car's here, and I'm going to shower before I go."

So Jericho left and drove to his apartment and fell into bed. Despite his exhaustion, though, sleep didn't come as quickly as he might have hoped. The situation with Kayla was a new problem, and he chewed it over for a while, but then his brain, as always, wandered back over toward Wade.

He was a suspect in whatever was going on with Kayla; clearly their shared childhood wasn't enough to make her off-limits in his machinations. And he was dragging Jericho into his web as well. He'd used Jericho as an alibi. He'd straight-out told him how he would manipulate people in authority. He was trouble, and there was just no way Jericho could pretend otherwise.

That kiss, though. That kiss. Wade was trouble, for sure. All different kinds of trouble.

CHAPTER 14

Jericho woke to his alarm midafternoon and called the school to be sure Nikki had picked up the kids. She had, which meant Elijah and Nicolette probably told her that someone else had been babysitting them when they'd woken up that morning. Someone Nikki didn't know. But Nikki hadn't called to scream at him, so either she was going to let it go or she was too mad to talk. He told himself he didn't care which it was, and then drove by her house on his way to the station. Nobody was outside, but the place wasn't on fire or anything, so things could be worse.

Garron was at the front desk when Jericho got to work, and gave him a glare that reminded him a bit too much of old times. "What's up?" Jericho asked, trying to sound breezy and confident.

"You hanging out with the feds, now?"

Of course he'd heard. The squad car had been parked at the motel where the feds were staying, and the woman who'd brought their food had been a local, and therefore certainly connected to Garron in a dozen different ways.

"Shows how dedicated to my job I am," Jericho replied. "I'll turn over every rock, no matter how slimy. Is the sheriff in the building?"

"She left a couple hours ago."

"On the job, or going home?"

"Home, I think."

Okay. Good. Kay was somewhere safe, *and* Jericho didn't have to be around her, feeling like a traitor for not telling her about the federal investigation. "Hockley here?"

"Your new friend? I don't keep track of the feds."

Yeah, Jericho should have known better than to ask. He jogged up the stairs to the offices, looked around to see who was in the building, and then realized he was at loose ends. He didn't have a patrol shift scheduled, and there was paperwork he could do, but nothing too pressing. He didn't need to be there, not unless the feds were going to let him in on whatever they were doing, and with Hockley nowhere in sight, he was probably shut out.

He sat down at his desk and frowned at the files he had stacked on it. Going over old records and reports had helped him find the drop house, but what good had that done? The feds had their forensic team go through it, but they hadn't found anything useful, or nothing useful they'd decided to share. And other than that one discovery, the files had given him nothing but a headache.

He grabbed his keys and jogged back downstairs. The sheriff's territory was too large for foot patrols to be effective, but there was still value in being out and about, being seen by the citizens. And value for him to see the people he was trying to protect.

Because that was what it all came down to. Protection. What did it matter if there were drugs being run through this territory? Well, if drugs were legal, maybe it wouldn't matter that much, or maybe it would even be a positive contribution to the economy. But while they were illegal, it meant trouble, especially when it was expanding like it was. It meant bikers and gangsters from the city setting things on fire, leaving bodies lying around, and otherwise making everything dangerous. And men who would commit arson and murder would commit other crimes too, of course. The people Jericho was sworn to protect were threatened by it all, and he couldn't look the other way.

He managed to keep himself from bringing Wade into the equation, or at least he thought he had. But somehow he found himself back on the edge of town, staring at the blackened wreckage of Kelly's. Wade had known it was going to burn, or hadn't been surprised or alarmed when it did. Had the Chicago crew told him they were going to do it? Threatened him, maybe, but given him time to make sure the place was empty? And then burned the bikers' clubhouse when it was empty too.

That would make it a kinder, gentler brand of organized crime, though, and something about that didn't feel right. There were three dead bodies in the morgue, and Chicago had responded with a building fire? Either they didn't value their people too highly, or they were de-escalating where escalation would have been expected. Or maybe it had just been a coincidence, lucky for the bikers and unlucky for Chicago, that the building had been empty.

Damn it, there was far too much he didn't know, and he wasn't supposed to be trying to find answers. He was supposed to be ... well, he was supposed to be doing more or less what he *was* doing, really. Driving around, patrolling, serving and protecting the citizens of Mosely in a highly limited context.

He pulled his phone out and tried to think of an excuse to make the call he wanted to make. He could just *ask* Wade who burned down his bar, and why. Because of course Wade would be happy to share that information, and he would be honest and forthright about the entire situation. Right.

He could ask what Wade knew about the bikers and the Chicago crew. Wade had given him basic information on that already, so maybe he'd be willing to share some more. It wasn't contrary to his interests, after all ...

But since when had that been enough to inspire Wade to do anything? Shit, Jericho was missing a detail again. Wade had told Jericho about the turf war, knowing Jericho would tell the feds. Civic responsibility wasn't high on Wade's list of personal qualities; he hadn't just been trying to help out.

Maybe he'd been trying to help Jericho. Maybe. *Definitely* he'd been trying to mess with him. That went without saying. But what else was there? Why did Wade want the feds to know about the turf war, and the Chicago gang's involvement?

That was when his phone rang with Kay's tone, and it was mostly a relief to answer it. "What's up?" he asked.

"Where are you?"

Well, that was a bit awkward, but there was a tension in her voice that made him answer without dissembling. "Kelly's. No one seems to be watching the wreckage anymore."

"I need you on a job."

"Where?" he asked, putting the phone on speaker and throwing the cruiser into gear. "What's going on?"

"The bikers are coming in. All of them, and we think extras from affiliate clubs. We suspect that at least some of the guests at the motel are from the Chicago crew, so that's their most likely destination, but we don't know for sure."

"Shit." He hit the lights. "You want me at the motel?"

"No. I'm heading to the motel, but it's just a guess. There really aren't enough unknown guests there for it to be a sure target. Hell, half of the rooms are taken by feds. So I want you on the edge of town. West end of Main. When the bikers come in, you tag along, and stay with them. There'll be other units there. If the bikers split up, coordinate so as many of them as possible get followed."

It made no sense. Ten o'clock on a Friday night, and the bikers were going to war, right in town? "They've got to be bluffing," he said, partly to himself. "They're not crazy enough to do this."

"Probably not. But it's a hell of a risk. If the Chicago crew don't respond well, something could flare up, and that could get out of control fast."

Jericho pulled off the road and turned his lights off. He hadn't been far from his assigned spot, and now he was ready. Waiting. And northwards, a stream of headlights was approaching, flowing toward town. "They're in sight," he reported. "Still a couple klicks out."

"The feds were watching the compound and are following from a distance," Kayla said. "The bikers are likely aware of them, but maybe not. You'll be the first uniformed presence they see."

"Me and a couple troopers," Jericho said as two state highway patrol cars pulled up on the opposite side of the road from him and turned around so they were facing the right direction.

"Okay, so you've got some backup. Use their radio frequency if you need to coordinate with them. Otherwise, just stay cool. We want the bikers to see you, but that's it. You're a silent reminder."

"We got an idea of how heavily armed the bikers are?"

"Those on bikes aren't packing too much. Handguns, probably. But they have a couple vans with them."

Jericho unlocked the M4 from the rifle rack and fit his key into the glove box to find the extra ammunition. The confrontation couldn't be allowed to come to a shoot-out—if it did, especially in town, he'd have already failed. But there was no sense in being unprepared.

"Most of the businesses around the motel are closed, and we're evacuating those that aren't," Kayla reported. He could tell from the noise in the background that she was at the motel, probably directing traffic. "The feds are with the Chicago crew, those who we know about and who would answer their doors, and they're working on protective custody, although shockingly, the visitors aren't too interested. State officials are aware, and we're getting a helicopter up here. But it's taking time."

Great, so the bikers could assault the jail instead of the motel, or even worse, catch the out-of-towners and the deputies all in transit between the two locations. There was nothing wrong with the plan; there just hadn't been enough time. If the bikers got into town now, they'd catch everyone at their most vulnerable.

The headlights were close, too close. Jericho took a deep breath, then put the cruiser in gear and pulled it across so it partly blocked the road. He turned the flashing lights on and saw the troopers' surprised faces in the blue and red glow.

"Our orders are to let them pass," one of the cops yelled out his window. "We've got nothing to arrest them on, and we don't have the manpower to arrest them all anyway."

"I'm not trying to arrest them," Jericho shouted back. He got out of the cruiser and walked around to the passenger side, then opened the door and made sure the M4 was on the seat, ready to go. He shouldn't need it. If he needed it, he was screwed, given the numbers he was facing, and he'd be taking the state cops down with him.

So he had to make sure this didn't escalate.

The pack had slowed when he turned his lights on, and the first two bikes had stopped now, about thirty feet from the cruiser. Jericho felt naked leaving the relative shelter of its protection, but he made himself do it. He'd started this stupidity, so now he would have to finish it.

"Mike," he said as casually as he could, nodding to the biker on the left. "Mr. DeMonte," he added, hoping he was correct as he saluted the other leader. "Sorry for the stop. I was just hoping we could have a quick talk."

"We're a little busy at the moment," Larry DeMonte said dryly.

"I appreciate that, and I'll try to be quick." Jericho was close enough now that he wouldn't have had to raise his voice if it weren't for the rumbling engines. Close enough that he'd be an easy target if one of the bikers decided to draw on him.

He needed to keep the interaction relaxed, so he forced himself to lower his shoulders. This was a couple of friends having a chat on the road, that was all. "I was just, well, I was just thinking about a conversation Mike and I had the other day. We were talking about how I saw my job, you know? What I thought was important? And the thing I said was most important was protecting locals. I don't give a good goddamn about out-of-towners, especially the ones who come here hoping for trouble. But I truly do hate the idea of any locals getting caught in the middle of a violent situation. You know?"

"A conversation you and Mike had?" Larry asked, and he didn't take his eyes off Jericho, which meant Jericho couldn't look at Mike. Shit. Had Jericho set off another episode in their power struggle? Not a good time.

"Just casual," Jericho tried. His shoulders were raised again, his legs almost aching with the instinct to run. "We went to school together, you know."

"I believe I was told about that, yeah." And finally he broke eye contact, turning to Mike and saying, "But I don't remember hearing that you two had talked about hopes and dreams and career ambitions."

"Granger said—" Mike started, but stopped when his uncle raised a hand.

"Under-sheriff Crewe, as I said, we're busy right now. And none of us are interested in playing your games. Are you going to try to stop us from getting past your car?" Larry spoke as calmly as if he were asking whether the daily special at the diner came with fries.

"No, sir, I have no reason to detain you. But as a courtesy, I was hoping you might let me know where you're heading. It ties in with that 'protecting the locals' idea."

"We're not planning to do anything to the locals," Larry said, with just the slightest stress on the last word. Not enough to make it sound like a threat against anyone, unfortunately. Nor would having grounds for an arrest give Jericho any ability to actually perform an arrest, not with this many bikers to deal with.

"I'm a bit worried about some getting caught in the cross fire." Jericho realized he was using Wade's slow, laconic cadence. It was strangely calming, at least until he remembered the damn *"Granger said"* that had come out of Mike's mouth before his uncle cut him off. "Is there some way I could help you, maybe? If you let me know what you're planning, I could try to—try to smooth the path. Try to keep things as low-key as possible."

Larry gave him a long stare, then said, "We're just going for a ride, Under-sheriff. I don't think we need any smoothing for that, do we?"

"Well, there are a lot of you, and it's dark, so drivers might be less likely to see you, and we all know that in a car versus motorcycle accident, the motorcycle is the one that comes out hurt." Yeah, he was trying a traffic-safety argument. If he got out of this alive, he'd laugh about it. Maybe. "I could escort you through red lights, if you wanted."

Larry's expression was unreadable. "We're fine on our own, Under-sheriff."

"And that courtesy element? The possibility that you might be willing to tell me where you're going just as a favor?" It was surprisingly difficult to abase himself in front of these men. He hadn't thought he had a lot of pride, but whatever he had sure objected to him asking for favors from bikers.

"I'm not sure I owe you any favors, Under-sheriff." Larry pointedly turned to Mike. "Do I?"

"No," Jericho said quickly. He wasn't sure what kind of trouble he'd caused for Mike, and was less sure why he cared, but he was getting increasingly used to acting on feelings he couldn't explain. "You don't owe me a thing. But this could be the first favor, you know? After this, I might owe you."

Larry's smile was tight. "I don't think we're interested in trading favors. Thanks anyway."

Then he revved his engine and pulled around Jericho, past the cruiser, and on into town. The rest of the pack followed him, the vans having to swerve onto the shoulder to get past.

Jericho jogged to the cruiser, ignoring the stares from the state troopers, and pulled the passenger door shut before reversing, shifting into gear, and heading after the bikers. "We're on our way in now," he said into the radio.

"Stay with them," Kayla said. Her voice was colder than he'd ever heard it, even the day before when she'd been threatening to fire him. "And stay in your damn car. That's an order."

"Kay, I—"

"I'm busy at the moment. If it's not relevant to the current situation, save it. We'll be debriefing when this is done."

He was pretty sure she muttered something after that, but he couldn't quite make the words out. He'd worry about it later, after the adrenaline had worked itself clear of his body, after his hands were able to hold the steering wheel with a grip that didn't make his knuckles ache.

But in the meantime, he could see the spotlight from the state helicopter shining down on Mosely, and he knew he'd given the state police at least a few more minutes to get in position, ready for whatever the hell the bikers were planning. He'd done his part, and if Kay didn't like it?

Well, clearly Kay didn't like it. But he'd deal with that later.

CHAPTER 15

"**W**hat have I said about your cowboy bullshit?" Kay demanded hours later, leaning over Jericho's desk, the tendons in her neck tight with anger.

"You aren't a big fan," he answered. "But, seriously, it bought us some time. The helicopter got there, you had a couple extra minutes to run the evacuation, and I don't know—maybe it was good for them to know we were watching."

"They would have known we were watching if you'd done as you were told and just followed them."

"Okay, so cross that off the list. But it did buy you a bit of time. I mean, tonight was a win, right? They cruised into town, circled around a little and got everyone's attention, and then they went the hell home. No shots fired, nobody dead. This was a good night, Kay. Why are you pissed off?"

She stared at him, then sank down into the chair across from his desk. "Do you understand what my job is?" she asked quietly. "Do you know my priorities?"

He'd been expecting bluster. "Uh . . . to serve and protect the people of Mosely County?"

"That's one of them," she agreed. Her voice was steel when she added, "And the other is to keep my people safe. My deputies, my under-sheriff, everyone who works in this building, they're *my* responsibility. Do you understand that?"

"I don't think it was all that dangerous, really—"

"And with that responsibility comes the expectation that they will follow my goddamn orders. Because I refuse to be in a situation where I'm responsible for someone I have no control over. I *refuse* to allow that to happen."

He wasn't sure what to say. "I didn't totally ignore your orders," he tried. "I mean, I went where you told me to go. And then I just . . . improvised. And it worked out okay! I'm fine!"

"No." It was past five in the morning, it had been a stressful night of watching the bikers cruise around town menacing her community, and Kayla was clearly exhausted. Jericho wanted to find somewhere soft for her to lie down and get some sleep. At least, that was what he wanted until she said, "You're suspended. Leave your badge and your keys on your desk. Your weapon is yours, so you can hang on to it, but make sure you're aware of the gun-permit laws for private citizens."

"What? Suspended?" Why was he so surprised? He'd never have gotten away with any of his rule-bending in LA. But this was Mosely, and Kay, and, damn it, "This was your idea. Me coming back here and helping you out. You *asked* me to do this." He'd been tempted to use the word *begged* but managed to restrain himself.

"Yeah, I did. That was when I thought you'd help me keep situations calm, not go out of your way to flare them up."

"I didn't flare anything up, not tonight! Maybe I didn't do much but buy some time, but maybe I calmed things down. But either way, I sure didn't make it worse!"

"You don't think so? You think the troopers aren't talking to everybody? You think the whole damn sheriff's department doesn't know that you ignored my orders, *again*? I've got the feds challenging my authority, and there's nothing I can do about that. But you? Damn it, Jay, I can do something about you. What you did was unnecessarily dangerous *and* made it appear like I can't control my department, and I won't accept either of those results. So, hell yeah. You're suspended."

Shit. Jericho'd been happy enough to lecture Hockley about respecting Kayla's authority, and then happy enough to defy her himself. He was a hypocrite, and the suspension was well-deserved. "Okay," he said. "Suspended. For how long?"

"Indefinitely," she said. "I'll think about it, and I'll call you in a couple days to see if we can figure out a better way for us to work together. But, Jay . . ." She just seemed sad, now. "If we can't find something better, then this won't be a suspension. It'll be a termination. Do you understand that?"

He nodded, and the polyester of his collar scratched against his neck. He'd be free of the beige and brown. That would be a good thing.

"What about the feds? The link to the bikers?"

"That's between you and the feds. If they want to continue using you, that's up to them. But you're not going to be doing it as my under-sheriff."

"I'm not sure how interested the bikers are going to be in working with me if I'm not part of the department anymore."

"That's not my problem."

And that was all there was to say. Jericho stood up and unclipped his badge from his belt, dug his cruiser and office keys out of his pocket, and tossed them onto the desk. It made a pretty small pile, but having the items off his body still left him feeling strangely, uncomfortably lighter. "You'll call," he said. "In a couple days."

"I will. And, Jericho, look—this isn't personal. As a friend, I can see why you did it, and I guess I—I don't think I can go all the way to saying I *appreciate* it, but whatever. I understand the instinct. But as your boss? I can't put up with that sort of thing."

He nodded. Maybe he could argue the details, but he understood the larger picture.

"Do you need someone to drive you home?"

He hadn't even thought about that. "No, I'll walk."

"It's been a long night, and you live across town."

"'Across town' doesn't really mean that much in Mosely. Thanks for the offer, though."

He felt like all eyes were on him as he made his way through the central office and down the stairs. Stupid, he knew. Anyone still at the station at that hour was trying to finish up their work and get themselves home to bed. They didn't know what had happened between him and Kay, and even if they did, they wouldn't have cared much.

But rather than making him feel better, that realization made him feel worse. He had no job, either temporarily or permanently, he had no family, other than the kids and their mother, none of whom gave a shit about him, and no real friends. Just the boss who was likely going to fire him and the criminal who . . .

The criminal who'd been mentioned by the bikers the night before. Jericho was on the street now, heading home, and he slowed his walk. They'd been talking about Jericho's conversation with Mike, and Mike had been about to use Wade to explain why the conversation had happened. Was that accurate?

It wasn't like Jericho hadn't known that Wade had ties to the bikers. The bastard seemed to have ties to every criminal in a five-hundred-mile radius. But he'd said something to Mike specifically about Jericho.

Maybe that wasn't what Jericho should be focusing on. He should be thinking about his job, and how to keep it, or else how to get out of it cleanly enough that he could return to LA without complications. Wade was no longer his problem, and neither were the bikers.

Neither were the feds, but when he got to his apartment building and saw the dark sedan waiting in front of it, he bent down and peered inside, and wasn't all that surprised when the interior lights flicked on and revealed Hockley behind the wheel. Jericho walked to the passenger side and waited for the window to roll down, but it didn't.

He was tired. Sleepy tired, but sick-of-it-all tired too. He wasn't currently working for any law enforcement organization; he didn't owe a damn thing to the feds. He should turn around and go inside and get some goddamn sleep.

Instead he reached for the handle, pulled the door open, and leaned down to peer inside. "Is it too much to hope that this is a coincidence, you being parked here?"

"Sorry. We need to talk." Hockley gestured with his chin toward the passenger seat. "Get in."

Jericho did, and they both sat there for a few breaths. Then Hockley said, "This is confidential. Not for sharing with your boss."

Jericho didn't bother mentioning his current lack of such an entity. "Okay."

Hockley sighed. "The bikers know you were working with us. They know about our deal."

"How? I mean, did Kayla's dad tell them?" It was crossing a line, as far as Jericho was concerned. Passing along little bits of information was one thing, but something like this? Telling criminals about someone working undercover was a damn good way to get the undercover person killed. But he'd think about that later. "How do you know what they know?"

"We have our own sources in their organization," Hockley said. "Which is, again, confidential information that you are not authorized to share."

Well, he might as well get it over with. "I don't think I'm going to be sharing all that much with Kayla anytime soon. I'm suspended."

"Yeah, I heard that."

It stung more than it should have. "Kayla told you already?"

"I just got off the phone with her. I was suggesting some work you might want to be involved in, and she clarified your status. She didn't give me details about what you did, though . . .?"

Jericho shrugged. "Intercepting the bikers was the final straw, but, you know, she wasn't too impressed with me going off with Mike in the first place." And his efforts in that regard had turned out to be useless, since Kayla had blabbed to her father and her father had sold the information to the bikers.

"Your suspension makes you less useful," Hockley said.

"Your concern for my welfare is overwhelming. But am I really any less useful than I already was? If the bikers know not to trust me, I wasn't going to be able to help you with that, anyway."

"I was thinking more in terms of helping with Kayla."

"Oh. Shit, yeah, I'm out for that too." Jericho sighed. "Sorry. I mean, she says the suspension wasn't personal. She says she's mad as my boss, not as my friend. So if shit goes down she might still talk to me."

Hockley gave him a long look. "And you're not mad at her? You still want to help?"

"I'm a bit mad at her. More for talking to her dad than for suspending me. But Kayla's Kayla, you know? We go back a long way."

"Kayla's Kayla," Hockley said thoughtfully. "And Wade Granger? Is Wade Wade?"

"Well, obviously, in a technical sense. But—" Yeah, Jericho needed some sleep. Why was he even trying to explain this to someone like Hockley? "It's like me and Kayla. There's professional, and there's personal. She can be mad at me about one, and care about me for the other. You know?"

"So you can deal with Granger on a professional level? Your personal loyalties won't interfere with that?"

"This is beginning to sound like something beyond a general inquiry."

"It might be, yeah." Hockley rubbed his face, and Jericho realized that the fed was probably as tired as he was. "It's too late to start drinking for real, but have you got coffee in your apartment? We should talk."

"Yeah," Jericho agreed. This wasn't his job, but he couldn't walk away from it. So he led the way up the walk to the apartment, and Hockley dragged along behind him.

CHAPTER 16

"Our guys have been poking around in Chicago," Hockley said once he was settled on the couch with a steaming mug of coffee in his hand. "Questioned Anders Pilman, tried to activate a few sources within his organization—that sort of preliminary action."

Hockley's casual hand wave made Jericho want to smack him. Like it was no big deal that Hockley could set things in motion way over in Chicago. "What'd they find out?"

"Primarily background, but some of it might be interesting to you. Did you know Pilman's been working with the bikers for a couple years now? Apparently a good chunk of what they bring across the border is his, or at least goes through him for distribution."

"No," Jericho said slowly. "I didn't know that. Wade made it sound like Pilman was new to the area."

Hockley's nod was carefully nonjudgmental.

"So what changed?" Jericho was mostly asking himself, but Hockley might already have an answer to the question. "They've been working together for years, and then three dead wiseguys and a burned clubhouse. What went wrong?"

"You want my personal working theory?" Hockley asked. "No proof of it, just what my gut says."

"Okay. Let's have it."

Hockley leaned back on the sofa cushions. "Wade Granger."

Jericho stared, and Hockley sat quietly, giving him time. "Motive?" Jericho managed to ask, but Hockley continued to wait. "Shit. You think Wade wants to take over the bikers' business? He wants to expand, I know that. Wants to use the information from that fucking thumb drive to build a damn empire. And maybe—yeah, maybe the thumb drive included the contacts in Chicago. Wade got in touch, said he wanted to do business . . ." Jericho tried to think the rest of it through, but this time Hockley jumped in.

"And Chicago said they already had good connections in this area."

"So Wade needed to make the connections not as good. Do you really think he has the mojo to do that?"

"I've been working on Wade Granger for the better part of a year," Hockley said. "He's interesting, because he doesn't have a large organization himself, which means, of course, fewer people to betray him. The few he does work with closely are intensely loyal. You know how these things go—we get most of our information from informants, plea deals—criminals telling us what other criminals are up to. In Wade's case, it's been hard to get much of anything. But we do know he's got connections throughout the region. We know he has greater power through influence than through actual foot soldiers. I mean, the man is one persuasive, charismatic son of a bitch, isn't he?"

There was no way Jericho was going to respond to that. "So Wade somehow used his influence over the bikers to make them kill three men from their partner organization? That goes beyond 'persuasive,' doesn't it?"

"We have no proof the bikers killed those men. Could have been Granger himself."

Could have been Granger. Could have been Wade killing three men. Jericho needed to do this. Needed to think of Wade, and three dead bodies, and a possible connection between them. Needed to keep himself from forgetting that there might be more bodies in Wade's past, and one of them might have been Jericho's father.

It wasn't as if Jericho hadn't killed people himself. Enemy combatants, a gangbanger in LA who'd shot first, and of course, the crooked feds not that long ago. Yeah, he'd killed, but only with good reason. Wade, executing three people just to stir shit up with the bikers? Just to make money? Jericho didn't want to believe it.

"What about his bar being burned down? That happened *before* the men were killed, right? So Chicago was already in town, already causing trouble."

"Seems likely," Hockley agreed slowly.

"That fire is about the only connection between Wade and any of this. Otherwise all we've got is a beef between criminal partners, which, let's face it, is not exactly unusual."

"But we do have the fire," Hockley replied calmly. "Same accelerant, same MO as the biker HQ fire. Unless there's a fourth player in all this, we can reasonably assume the Chicago crew set both."

"So what's your theory? Wade approached the Chicago crew, they didn't like his terms and burned down his bar to teach him a lesson? Okay, maybe. But killing the Chicago guys for revenge? No." He was relieved by how true the words felt as he said them. "Not for revenge. To send a message, to protect himself or his interests, to create an opportunity—maybe for any of those reasons. But three deaths as revenge for his bar burning down? A building that wasn't even valuable enough to have bothered to insure? No. That doesn't sound right to me."

"So what about those other motivations? Sending a message, protecting his interests, creating an opportunity. You see any of those here?"

"Not really."

"So say Granger didn't do it." Hockley twisted his mouth like he didn't like the taste of those words, but he continued anyway. "Say the three from Chicago went to see the bikers, since they were in town, and maybe they pissed the bikers off somehow."

"Maybe they tried to use Wade as a bargaining chip. Said they'd had a better offer from someone else so the bikers would have to match it or lose their business."

"Doesn't seem like enough to kill them over."

"Not unless it ties in with whatever's going on between Larry and Mike," Jericho mused. "Your source give you anything on that?"

"Confirmed the tension, didn't have details."

"Could he confirm the killings? Does he think the bikers did it?" Jericho frowned. "They were indirectly bragging about it, actually. Before you pulled up at the garage that day, one of them was saying something about how the bikers could take care of themselves. Definitely made it sound like he was talking about the three guys."

Hockley sighed. "Our guy thought they did it too. Wasn't sure why, though."

"Is your guy closer to Larry or to Mike?"

Hockley didn't answer right away. Finally, grudgingly he said, "Mike."

"And Mike was the one who took me out to be referee when he met with the Chicago guy. Maybe the Chicago crew are Mike's allies, and Larry's getting pushed out?"

"And pushing back." Hockley nodded. "Okay, yeah. I like that theory. Except it seems like they united long enough to come together for their little joy ride last night."

"Show of strength. Never hurts to appear strong, no matter who you are."

Hockley frowned and peered down at his watch. "I need to go shower and get to work. Look, the reason I came over to talk to you— it's been good to bounce ideas around, but the real reason—you think there's a chance Granger would talk to you about this? You think you can get anything out of him?"

"I'm sure as hell not going to be able to trick it out of him," Jericho said. "He's about ten times smarter than I am and about twenty times sneakier. If he tells me something, it'll be because he wants me to know it. He's not going to help just because I ask him to."

"He helped you before. Saved your life, as I recall."

"He got the thumb drive out of that deal. And I'm not saying he wouldn't save my life again, to be honest; I'd like to think he might. But that's totally different from giving me information he knows I'm going to use for a criminal investigation."

Hockley nodded as if he wasn't surprised by Jericho's answer. "It might still be worthwhile for you to talk to him. Don't tell him what we're up to or what we're thinking, just . . . give him the opportunity to tell you what he might want you to know. We can take whatever he says with a grain of salt, but even knowing the lies he wants you to believe could help us understand what his goals are."

"Wasn't too long ago you were throwing fits and warning me to stay the hell away from Wade," Jericho said.

Hockley nodded. "I'm not sure they were 'fits,' But, yeah, my approach has changed. You willing to change with it?"

"He's not going to give me anything useful."

"Everything's useful."

"So, what, I just give him a call and see if he wants to hang out?"

"I don't know—how have you contacted him in the past?"

"I don't, usually. I mean, I did when I needed his help when the kids got grabbed, but since then? He contacts me, not the other way around."

"You know what they say. Variety puts the spice back in a relationship. Maybe he's waiting for you to make the first move."

Jericho squinted at him. "Are you enjoying this?"

"I'm sleep-deprived." Hockley heaved himself to his feet. "Oh, and so you know—there was another big shipment across the border last night, and the Canadians let it go because they're building their own case up there and didn't want to mess it up to help us out." He shook his head. "I thought Canadians were supposed to be nicer than that. Anyway, they've got remote cameras, motion-activated, on their side of the border, and they sent us the images."

"Did the cameras show anything on our side?"

"Someone in a yellow slicker riding an ATV. Our guys went to the site and followed the ATV tracks, but it looks like the perp drove to the nearest logging road, loaded the ATV onto a trailer, and took off."

"Same crossing spot both nights?"

"Different spot. Same yellow slicker and ATV."

"A yellow slicker? Seems like a strange thing for a drug mule to wear."

"I don't think they have a dress code."

"Fair enough." Jericho frowned. "So, we've got two big shipments the last two nights. Maybe the biker parade last night was a distraction? We pulled in every law enforcement officer we could find to deal with that, and then it just fizzled out. Maybe the real action was going on at the border."

"Which suggests that it was either a biker at the border, or someone who can get the bikers to do what he wants."

Jericho tried not to remember the *"Granger said"* that had come out of Mike's mouth before his uncle cut him off. "Wade?"

"Couldn't be—he was with you night before last, wasn't he?"

"Not all night."

"We checked the time stamps. Wasn't him."

"So it could be completely unconnected, then."

"Could be," Hockley said, but he didn't sound convinced. He opened the apartment door, and once he was in the hallway, turned around. "Do what you can. Stay in touch. And if things with Kayla don't work out—" He grinned, sudden and bright. "Don't even think about applying to the DEA. We don't put up with cowboy bullshit."

Jericho snorted. "Thanks for your support."

Hockley gave a rough salute, and then he was gone.

Jericho closed the door behind him, then leaned against it. He'd contact Wade, sure. But he had a little digging of his own to do first.

CHAPTER 17

"Yeah, they're—they're interesting kids," Jericho said, keeping his smile fixed.

"They're little savages," Nancy Barcroft corrected, and she shifted around so her floral dress fell a bit more comfortably over her ample bosom and belly. "I couldn't believe the screaming when they first moved in next door. But . . . she pays me twice as much as anyone else I babysit for, so it's worth it. Mostly."

"And night before last—the night you saw me here with them— you were free that night? You take care of them pretty regularly, and you could have taken care of them that night?"

"Sure. When she was fresh out of the hospital I was over there every day with them. I don't know why she didn't ask me. Maybe you work for cheap?"

"Yeah, I worked for free that night. But it's not going to be a habit."

"Good. I can use the money, especially for the overnights. They're not great kids, but getting paid for sleeping? I'm okay with that."

Jericho nodded. "Last night, though. You only watched them for a few hours?"

"Yeah. She said she was going out to dinner. Not sure who with, though. She left here alone."

"And she was gone from about seven until ten or so?"

"About that."

"Okay, great. Thanks very much." He turned to leave.

"Uh, Deputy Crewe," she called after him. "Is this— I mean, I'm happy to help. But . . . I need the money from working for her. Is she going to be mad about me talking to you?"

"I don't know, for sure. What do you say we just keep it between you and me, just in case?"

She nodded. "That sounds good, Deputy. Thank you."

He only felt a little guilty about the "deputy" business. He hadn't identified himself as an officer, wasn't in uniform, wasn't driving a squad car—he couldn't help it if people in a small town knew who worked where. If she assumed he was on the job, that wasn't his fault.

Besides, he had bigger concerns to worry about. He pointed the Mustang downtown and found a parking spot in front of the hardware store. Another advantage of small-town living.

"Jericho!" The old man behind the counter greeted him with a smile. "Good to see you."

"Good to see you too, Mr. Appleby." He peered around the store for a moment, then saw the man restocking the shelves in the fasteners aisle. "Hi, Will!" he called, but there was no response.

"Sometimes he hears people, sometimes he doesn't," Mr. Appleby said with a resigned shrug. "Now, what can I help you with?"

"Uh, I don't actually need any hardware. But I was wondering—you know all the contractors around here, right? They come in and talk about things, jobs or whatever they're up to?"

"Sure. We're the only hardware store for thirty miles. Everyone comes through here."

"So, I'm wondering—did you ever hear about anyone doing any work at Kelly's? Before it burned down, I mean."

Mr. Archer raised an eyebrow and leaned forward with significantly more enthusiasm than he'd shown when he thought he was going to be selling something. "Interesting you should ask about that. I was talking to Tim Baylor a few weeks ago. He mentioned that he'd been in the place, talking to Wade Granger himself. Wade had been asking about getting some repairs done."

Jericho picked up one of the mini-flashlights from the display box on the counter and tossed it in what he hoped was a nonchalant way. "And what happened with that?"

"Tim's an honest man. He took a look at the job, and then he told Wade it didn't make sense to try to repair the place. Roof was a mess, wiring was terrible, there was mold and entire generations of mice in the walls, and it was never properly insulated—better to tear it down and start over."

Jericho's nod felt like his head was being jerked by a puppeteer's string. "And that was Tim Baylor who told you that? He's a local?"

"Lives north of town. Local enough."

So he could be found if necessary, and asked to testify. Not that Jericho truly believed he was ever going to get this case to a court of law. But he wanted to understand enough to try to minimize the fallout from whatever the hell was going on.

He said his good-byes and headed out of the store, then pulled out his phone. He had his theory, and now it was time to present it to the only person who could confirm or deny its accuracy. Not that Wade would actually admit to anything, or give Jericho any evidence. But as long as Jericho was able to read between the lines, Wade would give him his answer.

Which made it a bit frustrating when Wade's voice mail system picked up instead of the man himself. "It's Jay—I'd like to talk to you. Give me a call, please."

The message felt weak, but he had no idea how to make it stronger.

And, he realized as he stood there on the sidewalk, he didn't know what to do with his time, now that he was unemployed. So he made his way home and took a shower, and only when he was sagging under the steam and spray did he remember how long it had been since he last slept.

He'd left his phone on the bathroom counter so he'd be able to hear it if it rang, but he still checked it when he got out of the shower. Damn, he was antsy. Because of the investigation. Because he was curious, and wanted to see Wade's reactions to his theory. That was all.

The apartment was warm, with late-spring sunshine streaming through the windows, so Jericho didn't bother dressing. He stripped his bed and put clean sheets on it, slipped between the layers, and for about ten seconds, he was content. Clean, comfortable, and safe. Did he really need more than this?

His mind wouldn't cooperate, of course. Overtired and jittery, it insisted that he needed much more, a sense that he was having an impact on events. Justice? That wasn't a concept he thought about all that often. But some sense of control over his own destiny?

Hell yeah, he needed that. He didn't like being manipulated, not even if the manipulator was Wade Granger. Maybe *especially* when the manipulator was Wade.

He dozed off in the grumpy state and woke with the sun shining at a different angle through his window. He was still groggy and thought about going back to sleep, but then he heard it—a repeat of the sound that had woken him. Someone was knocking on his door.

Tempting to ignore it, until he remembered who might be looking for him. No time for a shirt or underwear, just jeans from the laundry basket, done up as he crossed to the front door. Nobody had buzzed to be let into the building, but if it was Wade—Jericho took a quick peek through the peephole. Yeah, Wade. He wouldn't have had much trouble getting someone to let him in. Slick bastard.

Wade raised his hand to knock again, and Jericho pulled the door open. Wade's fist froze in the air for a moment, then the fingers opened into a casual wave. "Jay. You got all dressed up for me?"

Jericho stepped back from the door, wishing he was wider awake, or more dressed, or hell, less dressed, but best not to think about that. "Where do you live, Wade?"

For a change, Wade seemed a bit surprised. "My home was recently destroyed in a tragic fire, the cause of which has not yet been determined by Mosely's finest."

"You lived at the bar?"

Wade stepped inside, glanced around the room, and said, "Well, I can only aspire to this level of luxury and refinement."

Jericho bit back his retort. He hadn't contacted Wade in order to fight about accommodations. "Must have made it a harder decision, then, to burn it down instead of repairing it. Or maybe not—I guess it would suck even worse to work *and* live in a shithole."

Wade raised his eyebrows. "I thought we'd already had this conversation. The bar wasn't insured, Jay. I didn't burn it down as part of an insurance scheme, no matter what your fed friend says."

"No, not as an insurance scheme," Jericho agreed, and he glanced at the clock on the microwave. "It's a bit early, but my schedule's so messed up I don't care. You want a beer?"

He turned and headed for the fridge, and he could *feel* Wade following behind him. He could feel the interest, the building excitement, the strange synergy between them that made it difficult to know which of them was feeling what. *This* was what Wade was after. Well, he'd probably wanted money or power or whatever the hell else from his criminal activities, but from Jericho? Wade wanted this. This conflict, this confrontation. Things had been simmering for too long, and it was time for them to boil over. Wade wanted that, and Jericho wanted it too.

They both stayed calm and controlled, though, as Jericho pulled out two bottles and twisted the lid off one before passing it to Wade.

"Your shoulder's healing well," Wade said. His body didn't move, but somehow his gaze made the puckered scar feel warm. "Does it still hurt?"

The topic change was disorienting. Damn it, Jericho was the one standing there with no shirt on—*Wade* should have been the one getting flustered. But Jericho didn't think he'd ever seen Wade flustered. "No, it doesn't hurt," he managed after a pause that felt far too long.

"Good," Wade said softly. "I'm glad." He took a drink. "So, you wanted to talk?"

It seemed stupid, now, like the big showdown at the end of a *Scooby-Doo* episode, but damn it, Jericho *did* want to talk. "You burned down your own bar," he said. "Not for the insurance, but the place couldn't have been worth much anyway, and making yourself into a victim threw suspicion off you, right?"

Wade raised his eyebrows. "Threw suspicion off me? As I recall, it brought the feds down on me with the rage of a thousand pulsing hemorrhoids."

"But the feds have always been looking at you. And since they assumed it was insurance fraud, it pointed them in the wrong direction. Meanwhile, you've been working on the bikers. You've been trying to set them off, either getting them to go to war with each other or with the Chicago crew. *You* burned down their clubhouse, trying to stir them up."

"I'm a very busy man, apparently," Wade said. His whole body was relaxed, his smile was pleasant—and his eyes were sharp. "But why would I do all this? Am I just an anarchist, bent on creating chaos?"

"You're doing it because you want to take over the bikers' territory," Jericho's voice wasn't as calm as Wade's, but he was in control of himself. And he took the time to sip his beer and watch Wade, and the lack of any reaction told him he was on the right track. "You've got the information from the thumb drive, but it's not all that valuable if other people are already using the drop spots and are already supplying the distributors, is it? It's a crowded marketplace up here, and a man needs to create his own opportunities."

"Haven't you been listening to the feds? I've been a criminal mastermind in these parts for some time now, as I understand it."

"A mastermind, maybe, but you haven't built an organization. You've been a one-man show. Now you've got Nikki, and maybe you're recruiting others. You know everybody, after all. You know who to tap when you need them."

"Nikki? She mentioned that you'd been making wild accusations, but, Jericho, I'm hurt. You think I'd seduce someone close to you into a depraved life of crime?"

Wade's eyes were dancing now; he was enjoying himself. And in a strange way, Jericho was too. "I absolutely think you would. I think you'd get a great deal of pleasure from it. And in Nikki's case, you've got the added benefit of the kids. You can use them to keep her loyal."

"I wouldn't threaten children."

"I never said that you would. And at first, I thought they made Nikki a *bad* choice as someone to trust, because if she ever got busted, she'd say whatever she had to, tell the cops any secrets she could think of, to get out and back to the kids." Jericho took a drink, his gut tightening pleasantly at the way Wade was watching him. Expectant. Intrigued. "But you've worked your way into their lives, haven't you? You're turning into a damn father figure. So if Nikki gets caught for something? She might rat out other people, but she won't say a word against Uncle Wade, not while Uncle Wade's the one on the outside, taking care of the kids she loves."

Wade was quiet for a while, and then he said, "I do actually like the kids." But he said it like an addition, not a contradiction.

"So you've brought in two big shipments while the bikers are running around like idiots, trying to figure out why the Chicago crew is attacking them, trying to deal with whatever other seeds you've sown—like Mike's decision to start agitating for leadership of the gang. But they haven't totally self-destructed, have they? Not yet, at least. They didn't attack the Chicago crew with all those cops buzzing around, not like you encouraged Mike to do." He took a drink and watched as Wade's half smile served as a subtle confirmation of their truth. "Jesus, Wade, you're playing with people's lives."

"It's the way of the world. Sometimes bad things happen to— well, in this case, the bad things happened to bad people. So I'm not going to get too upset about it."

"And the three dead wiseguys?" Jericho demanded. He was ready to take his pet theory out for a walk. "The bikers killed them, but Chicago hasn't really retaliated; even if they set the fires, a damn building fire doesn't make up for three deaths. And I have my doubts about the building fire. So instead of a real retaliation we've got a few wiseguys in town not doing much. The bikers think there are more, but that's because you've told them there are more, right? I'm still trying to figure out why there *hasn't* been a real retaliation from Chicago—you got anything you want to tell me on that front?"

"I can neither confirm nor deny any of your outrageous conjectures. But I am enjoying the story you're telling. I truly am." Wade stepped closer. "Do you know that when you get passionate about something, your skin flushes? Not a lot. But I'm good at noticing things about you. It starts on your face, and spreads down your neck." He reached out and ran his fingers through the air, two or three inches from Jericho's body, to show the path he was talking about. "And then it's interesting. How it conforms to the same pattern as the hair on your chest. Wide across the top—" and his hand was a little closer, now, close enough that Jericho could almost feel it "—and then it narrows into a thin line as it goes lower. Down over your belly, all that warm skin, and then down—" He looked up, his expression serious. "In the name of science, Jay, I think you should take off your pants and let me see how much farther it goes."

God help him, Jericho was truly tempted. But he made himself snort, and it sounded pretty good, only a little breathy at the end. "I hadn't realized you were interested in science." He took two big swallows of beer, emptying the bottle, and then said, "The bikers killed the wiseguys. Not you. But they killed them because Chicago asked them to. Right?"

"How would I know about any of that?"

"Of course you wouldn't know. But just in theory—what would make Chicago want three of their guys dead? Why would that happen?"

"In theory?" Wade's expression was hard to read, but Jericho knew what was going on. Wade wanted to show off. Wanted to *play*. "I can only imagine what conflict there must be within a criminal organization like that. I wonder if there was some sort of problem with—I don't know, maybe an information leak? Maybe one of the soldiers was talking to the cops, and the brass wasn't sure exactly who it was?" Wade's shrug was exaggerated. "This is the kind of thing *you'd* know about, Under-sheriff. It's not my area."

An informant. Damn, it made sense. "So Chicago sent them out here, the bikers took care of them, and you let us think it was part of a fucking turf war so we'd worry about what they were up to instead of worrying what *you* were up to."

"And what is it that I was up to, again?"

"Bringing two big shipments across the border. Big enough that the Canadian cops knew about it and tipped us off. Maybe we could have done something about them if we'd been paying attention. You had the bikers tricked into thinking there *was* trouble with Chicago, even though they killed the guys by request, so they took their little tour and threw us off."

"And I did this the last two nights? That's what you're saying? You're forgetting about how you and I were together on the first one of those nights? I couldn't have been up at the border, because I was in Nikki's kitchen, with you." Wade stepped closer. God, he was beautiful. *And a criminal.*

Jericho stepped away. "Yeah, that night you were with me, and Nikki was at the border. The next night, Nikki was out on the town, making sure she was noticed, and you were at the border. You're about the same height, and you both wore some ridiculous yellow slicker to make it look like you were the same person. I mean, seriously, Wade, who wears a yellow slicker in the Montana woods? You don't think that was overkill?"

"Are you giving fashion advice, now? That's kind of you."

"Where does it go from here?" Jericho lifted his bottle, remembered it was empty, and set it on the counter behind him. Damn, he'd let Wade back him up that far? He was all the way into the kitchen, with no more room to retreat. And possibly no willpower to resist if Wade came in any closer.

"Maybe another beer?" Wade suggested. "Maybe fewer clothes?"

"Not where does *this* go from here! Where does your *plan for the bikers* go from here?"

"Oh, that." Wade shrugged. "I'm sure it'll take care of itself. In the meantime I'm thinking of taking a little vacation. I happened to hear that an old friend of mine just lost his job, and I thought maybe he'd like to do something with me. We could go hiking, or fishing, or—" he cut his eyes toward the bedroom with a too-obvious leer "—or we could stay in."

Jericho ordered his body to ignore the hint of a growl in Wade's voice. "What are you up to? Are you— Fuck, Wade, are you doing your fucking reverse-psychology thing? You want me to go somewhere so you're acting like you want me to stay? Or is it another double reverse, and really you want me to stay?"

"Why don't we focus on the 'want you' part, and ignore the rest of it?" Wade didn't move any closer, but his face softened almost imperceptibly, lost the polished sheen of his façade. "Don't you ever wish it could just be you and me again? Just us, without all the complications? This could be our chance. You're not a cop right now, and I'm—" He shrugged. "To the best of my knowledge, I'm not currently doing anything illegal."

Jericho bit back a sound that was half snort, half something that was far too close to a giggle. Damn, he was keyed up.

Wade's smile was sweetly familiar. "You knew I wasn't going to tell you about business, so there's no bugs in the apartment. Nobody listening. Nobody around. Just you, and just me."

And then he moved closer and ran the back of his knuckles along the line of hair on Jericho's belly. Jericho's abs contracted, almost a shiver, and goose bumps rose. Wade's scent was in his nose, and he gripped the edge of the counter so tightly his knuckles ached. He was breathing too fast, and it was making things worse, with each breath bringing more of Wade into his lungs, his body.

I planned this, he realized in that distant part of his brain still capable of coherent thought. Wade was right. There'd been nothing to gain by having this confrontation; he'd known Wade wouldn't make a confession, not in any way that could be used against him. Wade hadn't been the only one who'd wanted to play, and to show off.

But Wade was even closer now, his expression was . . . wrong, somehow. It was too cold, the teasing warmth vanished as if it had never been there. Jericho shivered, suddenly feeling exposed.

"You've got it all figured out," Wade said quietly. "But you haven't told anyone else, yet. You didn't want to do that until you were sure you were right. You've got a list of felonies you think I've committed or conspired to commit, and you and I are the only ones who know about any of it. And as long as you don't leave this apartment, things will stay that way."

Jericho couldn't speak. His throat was too tight, but even if he'd managed to force some sound out, he didn't have any words. Wade. It was Wade, his old friend, his old lover. Wade the career criminal, the man who'd probably already killed one Crewe over business. And Jericho was half-naked, his gun safely stowed in the drawer beside his bed across the room.

"You're thinking now, Jericho," Wade said. No heat in his voice but no warmth either. "You're realizing how vulnerable you are." He reached calmly under his jacket, and when his hand reappeared it was holding a Beretta 9mm. His grip was loose and casual, the barrel pointed at the floor, but in Jericho's general direction. Wade kept his eyes locked with Jericho's. "Two shots. That's more than I need, and it's easy to get away with. Your neighbors will hear, but they won't be able to pinpoint the source of the noise. If they call the police—well, you tell me, Under-sheriff. How fast will the sheriff's department respond to the possibility that maybe somebody fired a gun somewhere in town—or maybe there was a backfire, or someone was playing the TV too loud?"

"You're not serious," Jericho said. They were terrible last words, but they were all he could think of. "You're not going to do this."

Wade stared at him. "I'm holding a fucking gun. And I have every reason to want to shut you up."

"Killing a cop? How much extra heat would that bring down on you?"

"Like the fed I killed last month?" Wade actually licked his lips as if savoring the memory. "Can't say I've felt any repercussions from that. And dead cops aren't that big of a deal these days, not in Mosely."

"Kay would make it a big deal."

"Kay's in the process of kicking you off the force. I'm sure she'll be upset, but she'll get over it."

Jericho needed to move. To attack. He was stronger than Wade, he could overpower him if he got the chance. But Wade had always been faster than Jericho. Too fast. And Wade had the gun half-raised, now. Pointed at about gut-height, but still off to the side.

Wade wasn't pointing the gun directly at him. Not yet. If Jericho moved, Wade could aim fast enough. But Wade knew his gun-safety rules. Never point a gun at someone you don't want to shoot.

That was all Jericho had, but he needed it to be enough.

"You won't do it." He couldn't let himself think about Eli, couldn't wonder if his father had felt this same sense of trust immediately before Wade pushed him off the damn cliff. "It's me, Wade. You and me, just like always. I have no fucking idea how things are going to end between us, but I know it's not going to be like this. And you know it too." *Please, please let him know it too.*

Wade stared at him and raised the gun higher, aimed it closer. "You're too confident, Jay. You're counting on shit you shouldn't be counting on."

"Counting on you, Wade?" God, this had to work. "Okay. Fine. Point the fucking gun at my face, and look at me while you're doing it. Tell me I'm wrong to believe you won't hurt me. Tell me that and pull the fucking trigger."

Wade didn't move the gun. Didn't raise it, didn't lower it.

Jericho had no more words. And for once, Wade didn't seem to have a speech.

Slowly, so slowly, Jericho reached his hand out. Not toward the gun, but toward Wade. The back of Jericho's knuckles traced along Wade's arm, the one at his side. Then up to his neck, down along his chest. Familiar, foreign territory. Jericho let himself exhale. "Put the gun away, Wade. It's a bit of a mood killer."

Then Wade moved. As fast as Jericho had known he could, but his body, not his gun hand. Forward, into Jericho, shoving him backward, his mouth finding Jericho's in a desperate, bruising kiss that felt like a question, a demand, and a statement. But not a threat.

Jericho lost track of where the gun was—it didn't matter anymore. He gripped Wade's shirt, pulled him in even though they were already tight against each other, and kissed back, just as hard.

But Wade pulled away. "You're killing me," he gasped. "You can't wander around town thinking you're fucking safe." He tucked his gun back under his jacket, giving him two hands for grabbing Jericho by the shoulders and shaking him. "Getting in Mike DeMonte's car after I told you he was a fucking psychopath? Thinking you're invincible or something?" He jerked his chin toward the healing scar on Jericho's shoulder. "You're not bulletproof, Jay."

"No. Not bulletproof. But you were there—you shot a fed, you got me out of there."

"You can't— Fuck, I can't. I can't always be there. You can't count on me. You can't assume you're safe around me."

"I'm safe around you. And it's not your job to keep me safe anywhere else." The adrenaline was still coursing through Jericho's body, but it was moving differently now.

"Fuck," Wade said, maybe to himself, and his shoulders slumped in defeat. "So, what now? You go tell your theory to the feds?"

Jericho nodded. "Pretty soon, yeah. But first—"

Wade was ready for him. Wade of the laughing eyes, the generous mouth. Wade who knew Jericho well enough to anticipate his lunge and catch it, spin it, turn it into something closer to a dance. Wade who allowed himself to be pinned against the wall, gave Jericho's brain a chance to at least partly catch up to what his body had just done, and then tucked his warm fingers inside the waistband of Jericho's jeans.

"Shit," Jericho murmured, but that was all he could manage before Wade's lips were on his, Wade's tongue lapping protestations away before Jericho could form the impulses into words.

This was stupid, and Jericho knew it, but that didn't matter. Wade's jacket fell to the floor, a dull thud making it clear that the gun had fallen too. Jericho's fingers were quick and sure on the buttons of Wade's shirt, his earlier apprehension gone now that he was actually doing something he'd wanted to do for so long. He pushed the gray fabric off the golden skin of Wade's shoulders, pulling his head away to watch, almost hypnotized, as its beauty was revealed. Wade had been a skinny kid and he was still a lean man, but there was a layer of tight, hard muscles stretched across the familiar bones now. The dusting of dark hair was new too, and Jericho wanted to slow everything down so he could explore more thoroughly.

Then Wade's fingers curled just a little in Jericho's waistband, just enough to remind him how tight his jeans had become and how simple it would be to fix that discomfort.

Stupid! Stupid! a distant thought warned him, but it was easy to ignore that when he could run his hand over the front of Wade's shirt and make the man bite back a moan.

Jericho propped one forearm on the wall beside Wade's head and kept their faces close together while his other hand skimmed down Wade's chest again and then flipped open the button on his jeans. Jericho was in control now, and it was about damn time. He yanked the zipper down, and that was all the room he needed. Quickly, efficiently, he slid his hand inside Wade's underwear and eased the elastic waist down to tuck under his balls.

There wasn't time to appreciate the view, not when something more important was going on. Jericho closed his fist around Wade's shaft, so intent on the task that he barely noticed what Wade was doing until his own pants were open and his own cock was wrapped in a tight, warm grip. Of course. This was Wade; he wouldn't give up without a fight.

They both knew the game. It had been a while since they'd played it, but some memories never faded, especially not ones this sweet. Jericho slid his lips along Wade's jawline, up behind his ear, searching for the sensitive spots that must still be there. He felt Wade's body jerk, heard him swear, and knew he was doing a good job.

He tried to ignore Wade's insistent hand on his cock, gasped when fingers closed around his nipple, but kept fighting for control. This was what it always came down to, after all. Which of them could maintain control the longest?

"God, you're driving me crazy," Wade whispered. Not an admission: a strategy. "I fucking missed you, missed the way you feel, the way you make me feel. Your cock, I can feel it leaking for me; you want me just like I want you."

Shit. It was a *good* strategy. The words, the tone, the fact that it was Wade. Jericho was in trouble if he didn't up his game.

With his free hand, he grabbed what he could of Wade's short, dark hair, using his grip to yank Wade's head up, hard enough that it bounced off the wall. But that was fair, that was good, even. Wade had always liked things rough. Jericho slid his mouth down over Wade's throat, using teeth more than lips, now, scraping and nipping and searching for the next spot, the next reaction. Wade's hand left Jericho's nipple and stretched around behind him, down to the crack of his ass, then over the cheek before he dug his fingers in, dragging Jericho forward into him.

Jericho couldn't hold back his gasp, and Wade chuckled, then cried out as Jericho bit down, finding the fleshy part of Wade's shoulder, the same spot as the bullet scar on Jericho's body.

"Oh, you bastard," Wade choked. "You fucking cheater, you— Oh, fuck, Jay—oh—" And then the words didn't make sense anymore, just turned into gasping and moaning.

If Wade hadn't lost control of his hands, Jericho would have followed him right over the cliff about a second afterward, but as it was, he got the full victory. He got to stand there and watch Wade fall apart, and then got to watch as Wade recovered, realized the situation, and slipped easily, gracefully to his knees.

"Never been much of a punishment," he murmured, and then he flicked his tongue out over the head of Jericho's cock.

It was almost enough, just that, but Jericho managed to hold himself together, shift around so the wall was supporting him better, and wait.

Wade didn't disappoint. A few teasing licks, a hand reaching behind to cup Jericho's balls, and then the full slide. Deep and tight and *Jesus*, the suction. Jericho fought to keep his eyes open, tried desperately to control his body, but Wade showed no mercy and Jericho couldn't last. "Wade," he warned, but there was no lessening of Wade's assault, and Jericho let himself surrender.

It had been too long. Too long with nothing but his hand, sure, but beyond that, too long since it had been *Wade*. Jericho came hard, his whole body tight and then loose and then tight again, every muscle straining in ecstasy.

When he finally managed to open his eyes and look down, Wade smiled back up at him. "I really did miss you, Jay."

Fuck. Jericho stumbled away from the wall, away from Wade, pulling his pants back together as he went. What the hell had he just done?

He made it to the fridge, opened it, and pulled out a beer just because he needed something to do with his hands, then reached for another and passed it to Wade without making eye contact.

They stood there in the kitchen, Jericho staring at his beer and far too aware that Wade was watching him with his trademark ironic smile.

"You okay?" Wade eventually asked.

Jericho frowned at him. "What did you do with the drugs, Wade?"

Wade raised both eyebrows. "Drugs? What drugs?"

"The drugs you brought across the last two nights. I don't think you've got things set up with the Chicago crew, yet. If you did, the bikers would be after your head, right? So you haven't got a distribution network big enough to handle that quantity of product. You've got it stashed somewhere?"

"Is this your idea of pillow talk?" Wade's mask was back, his cool, sardonic face showing no signs of strain. Good. Naked Wade had been a bit too much for Jericho to handle.

"I don't see any pillows, so this is just talk."

"You aren't even going to let me enjoy the afterglow?" Wade edged closer and lowered his voice. "You expect me to just forget what it feels like to have your cock in my mouth, down my throat, what it tastes like, what it *sounds* like when you come?"

"Stop it," Jericho said sharply. He did not need to get turned on again, couldn't afford to repeat this mistake. Maybe he'd had the power for about five seconds—five glorious, intoxicating seconds—but of course it was all back to Wade now. "This isn't over. I mean—" He needed to pull himself together and start making sense, but instead he waved vaguely around the apartment. "*This* is over. What happened here, that's done. But you're not done with what you're doing out there. You aren't just sitting back and letting the situation rest. You haven't got what you wanted yet."

There was a moment when Wade seemed almost—well, not *hurt*, probably, but almost disappointed? Then he shrugged, glanced at the clock on the microwave, and looked back at Jericho. "I admit I haven't checked to see how it went. But . . . I'm pretty sure it's over now. Or at least, this stage is over."

Jericho stared at him, and Wade stood waiting, his casual expression belied by the sharp excitement in his eyes.

"What have you done, Wade?" Jericho asked, his voice almost a whisper.

Wade just smiled. "If I've done it right, you'll figure it out soon enough."

CHAPTER 18

It was all over the radio, and news crews came up from Billings and Helena to cover the press conference. Jericho was there, in the back of the crowd, watching as it unfolded on the steps of the sheriff's office.

The bust was the result of a joint federal task force, working in the area for several months, meticulously building a strong case—Hockley was in his element as he went through the details, managing to be boring despite the clear excitement he was trying to keep under control. Many members of an outlaw motorcycle club, including the entire leadership, were facing multiple charges related to trafficking in various narcotics, importing narcotics with the intention of trafficking, and illegal weapons. Valuable evidence had also been gathered that would contribute to building a case against members of the organization for the recent triple homicide.

According to the timeline the feds presented, the bust had been carried out the day before, while Wade had been in Jericho's apartment.

Jericho listened to the questions from the media, wishing he could jump in and ask a few of his own. But maybe he didn't want to hear the answers. Or maybe he didn't need to hear them.

"It's all wrapped up nice and tidy," he heard a familiar voice say, and half turned to find Kayla at his elbow.

"Seems like," he agreed carefully. "How come you're down here instead of up there taking some credit?"

"Not much credit to take, not on this one. The feds never let me in, so I didn't do much on this at all."

"I know the feeling."

Her look was quick and sharp, but he shrugged it off. She was tough.

They stood together and watched the rest of the press conference, and when it was over Hockley jogged down the concrete steps, shoulders loose and step confident. He was the conquering hero, descending from the great heights to share a moment of his time with the peasants.

"Wade set this up," Jericho said as soon as Hockley was close enough to hear quiet speech.

"What?" Hockley said. "No, I think we were overestimating Granger's involvement in it all. I mean, I'm sure he's guilty of a lot of *other* crimes, but this one—"

"He set it up," Jericho said. He didn't need to argue this, not when he knew it with such certainty, but it felt like his responsibility to at least tell Hockley the truth. What the feds did with the situation afterward wasn't Jericho's problem.

"We can talk later," Hockley said, and clapped Jericho's shoulder in a way that probably looked like a good-natured dismissal. But Jericho felt the extra squeeze and got the message. They could talk later, when Kayla wasn't listening.

Hockley strode off, likely to glad-hand whoever else he could find, and Jericho was left there with Kayla. His boss, sort of. His friend, definitely. He understood the reasons why she couldn't know about her father's activities, and he more or less agreed with them. Just like he understood the reasons for his suspension. But damn it, he didn't like being on the outside, not aware of what was going on with her, not knowing how to help. His suspension was interfering with his ability to help her out, in more ways than the obvious.

"I was out of line," he said quickly. "That—that cowboy bullshit. It felt right, and it worked out okay, but that's not the point. I need to trust your decisions and follow your orders. And I *do* trust your decisions, Kay. I promise. That was— I was wrong. Sorry."

She frowned at him suspiciously. "And how will we be sure the same mistake won't happen again?"

"I don't know. I mean, obviously I'll try to be more aware of what I'm doing. I'll try to take less initiative, and be a better follower? What are you looking for?"

"I guess I'm looking for a reason to trust *you*. It's great that you trust me—" She stopped. "Okay, that came out sounding sarcastic, and it shouldn't have. It *is* great that you trust me. I appreciate that. But it has to go both ways, doesn't it?"

"Yeah, I get that. But I'm really not sure what— I mean, that's your thing, not mine. You trusting me or not is going to come from you, so I kind of need some hints so I know what will make you feel better about all this."

"Let's not say 'feel better' as if I'm hormonal or something and you need to humor me, okay? You screwed up, Jay. This isn't about what I feel, it's about what I know."

He tried to restrain his frustration. "Okay, so what's it going to take to make you know you can trust me?"

Her expression softened. "You know I'd trust you with my life, right? I mean, I trust your intentions, absolutely. I know you're on my side. I just—" She stopped, then frowned. "Shit, maybe that's enough. Things have to calm down now. No more biker bullshit means no more *reason* for you to get reckless."

Well, he wasn't sure he quite agreed with that, but apparently his cautious nod was enough for her.

"Okay. So, we'll give it another try. *One* more try. You'll remember that I'm responsible for your safety, and you'll act in a way that will *not* give me multiple heart attacks."

"Yes, ma'am."

She nodded, then said, "Good. That's settled. So, in your first duty as reinstated under-sheriff, you'd better go track down Hockley and have that conversation he didn't want to have with an audience. If they aren't going to talk to me, talking to you is better than nothing."

He snorted. "You don't miss much, do you?"

"I'm missing whatever's up their asses about sharing information. But, no, I'm not totally clueless."

"I'll see what I can do," he said. "And, Kay—I've got your back, okay? Always."

"You'd damn well better," she grumbled, and then she turned away and skirted around the crowd on the way into her station.

CHAPTER 19

"It was a clean bust," Hockley told Jericho. They were in Jericho's office, both with cups of coffee, with the door closed. "Totally by the book. What makes you think Granger had anything to do with it?"

"You got a search warrant, went in, and found narcotics and illegal weapons," Jericho said. "Tidy. What'd you use as probable cause for the search warrant?"

"Surveillance," Hockley said. He sounded testy. "We had a guy on the hill across from the warehouse they've been working out of. He saw an ATV with a yellow slicker on it parked behind the building. We had a reliable informant who told us he'd been contacted by the bikers with an offer to sell considerable quantities of various narcotics. We're working on chemical analysis to connect the narcotics with those that crossed the border on two nights this week. We had—damn it, Jericho, we had plenty! What the hell are you worrying about?"

"The bikers were only in that location because Wade burned down their old headquarters," Jericho said tiredly. "He used the fire to stir up the bikers and make them think they were under attack from Chicago, but he also used it to flush them out of their safe hiding place. You never could have gotten that kind of surveillance at the old spot."

"Okay, that sounds pretty paranoid, but even if it's true, there's no way anyone would ever believe Granger was operating as an agent of the police, so it doesn't invalidate our search. We're still fine."

Jericho nodded. "He parked the ATV there too, or arranged for someone else to park it there. A yellow slicker? He was waving a fucking flag at us, telling us where to look."

"Do you have any proof of that? Any actual evidence that connects Granger to the ATV?"

"No," Jericho said. "Of course not. And I don't have any proof that he was the one who brought the shipments across the border, or that he planted the drugs at the bikers' warehouse. But I know that he did."

"Planted the drugs?"

"If you connect those drugs to the ones that came across the border, then, yeah, he planted them. Even if you can't make the connection, why the hell would the bikers stockpile that much quantity in a location known to police? It makes no sense, not unless Wade stashed the stuff there. Hell, he could have done it that first night, with the first shipment, while the bikers were running around worrying about the fire. He doesn't have an alibi for the time after he left Nikki's, does he? The bikers moved into a warehouse that was *already* storing drugs."

"Jesus Christ, Crewe." Hockley flopped back in his chair and stared at Jericho with disgust. "What the hell do you expect me to do with all this? I can't go to the goddamn US attorney and tell him to drop the charges because some backwoods under-sheriff thinks his ex-damn-boyfriend is truly responsible for the crime!"

Apparently Hockley's intel had gotten a little more precise than it had been the last time he'd been throwing around accusations about Jericho's sex life. "No," Jericho said mildly. "I don't expect you to do that."

"So, what are we talking about, then?"

"This is a federal case. You guys pushed your way in here and took over and that's your right. But now that it's gotten complicated? It's still a federal case. It's still your damn problem, and it's not my job to tell you what to do with the information I've given you."

"It's not information, it's fucking paranoia!"

"You've been investigating Wade Granger for the better part of a year, Special Agent Hockley. You really think anything I'm suggesting is beyond his capabilities, or not in keeping with his character?"

Hockley stared at him for a few long moments, and then spoke in a more controlled tone. "You talked to him, then? He— I know, he didn't confirm anything. But he let you know this was what he did?"

"No. I'm putting a few things together."

"But there's no evidence, not even a half-assed, hinted-at, his-word-against-yours confession."

"Nope." Jericho tried to smile. "If it makes you feel any better, he *did* give me a half-assed, hinted-at, his-word-against-mine confirmation that the bikers took out those three wiseguys. One of them was an informant, maybe? That sound right? And Chicago sent them out to be taken care of. Bikers were doing their partners a favor."

Hockley leaned forward. "Granger actually *told* you the guy was an informant? He had that information?"

"He had the information, but he didn't actually tell me. He presented it as a hypothetical."

"Of course he did."

"But you're able to verify that much, at least? One of the Chicago crew *was* working with law enforcement?"

Hockley gave him a look. "I'm afraid I'm not at liberty to share that information."

"Yeah, that was good. That's just how Wade tells me things. You guys have more in common than you think."

Hockley snorted. "Anything else I should know?"

"Not something you should know, but something you already do. You having any luck finding the army of foot soldiers Chicago would have sent over if they were truly planning to go to war with the bikers? You finding *any* sign that we had more than a few visitors from the Chicago organization?" Jericho waited for a reply, and when he only got a frustrated glare, he shrugged. "Maybe they're good at hiding. Or maybe they never fucking existed."

Hockley stewed for a few moments, then said, "Okay, off the record, off the books. What am I supposed to do with this conversation?"

"On or off the record, I have absolutely no idea."

Another snort. "Yeah. Shit." He took a deep breath, then pushed himself to his feet. "I'm going to talk to my boss. I'm going to tell her what you said, and tell her that you're an old—an old friend of the suspect's. And she'll tell me that there's absolutely no evidence of any damn thing and I need to keep my mouth shut and not stir up trouble, and that's what I'll do."

"So that's what I'll do too."

Hockley squinted at him. "And we'll both just sit back and watch these guys go to jail for drugs they weren't trafficking?"

"We sat back and watched them *not* go to jail for drugs they *were* trafficking. I'm not saying it's a perfect system. But, I'll be honest: I'm not going to lose sleep over this."

"No, *you're* not, because you've done all you can!"

Jericho leaned back in his chair and rested his feet on the desk. Suddenly his beige polyester wasn't quite so scratchy. "You're in charge, Special Agent. Enjoy."

The biker arrest was the biggest news Mosely had seen in a good while, and everybody seemed to have an opinion they wanted to share. Jericho ducked as much of the conversation as he could, spending more time than ever working out in the department gym or running through the mountain trails. If he was exhausted enough, he could usually have a beer in the shower when he got home and then fall asleep without torturing himself with thoughts of Wade Granger. He could usually forget the man's cocky, maddening grin; his endless manipulations; the feel of his body hard and hot against Jericho's—

Shit. He clearly needed to add to his running time.

But that didn't end up working too well, because one evening about a week after the press conference, he was headed up his usual trail along the crest behind the high school, and he saw a too-familiar shape in black and gray leaning against a tree. Waiting for him.

Jericho slowed to a walk. He thought about turning around, but he'd be damned if he'd run away from Wade Granger. And maybe he wanted to know what the man had to say for himself. And maybe he was unable to resist temptation. "What are you doing out here?"

"I'm enjoying nature. It's a beautiful evening, isn't it?"

"It is," Jericho said, and kept walking. It would have been better if he'd never stopped running, probably. He should have breezed by with a nod or with nothing.

Wade fell in beside him. "You mad at me, Jay?"

"Mad? I'm not sure that's the word I'd use." He stumbled a little, then turned to look at the man beside him. "You mad at *me*, Wade? Is that what—" No, Wade had always taken joy in manipulating others. He was eager to drag Jericho into his games, to torture him, because he was a cop, not because—not because— "I left you here. Left you behind."

Wade was walking faster now, keeping his eyes on the path in front of them. It seemed like he wasn't going to answer, but finally he glanced over and said, "Fifteen years." A quick, almost fragile smile. "I thought you were going to come back in about a week. I thought—most of the time, I thought—you were going to get out there in the real world and realize it was missing something. Something you fucking *needed*."

"I asked you to come with me." It sounded like he was making an excuse, and that made him mad. "You seriously thought I could stay here? With— Jesus, with all of it? You think I wouldn't have turned out—" He caught himself, but it was too late. Wade always knew what Jericho was going to say before he said it.

"Turned out like me," Wade said. His smile was hard. "I'm glad you're happy with who you are, Jay. That's nice." He turned around and took a few steps back the way they'd come, then stopped and looked back at Jericho. "But while you're living your righteous life, all respectable and proper? You should remember me. You should remember how it feels to have my hands on you, my *mouth* on you. You should remember me fucking you, and you fucking me, all the ways we took care of each other back when we were kids. You should ask yourself: if it was that perfect then, when we didn't know what the hell we were doing, how much better would it be now?"

Jericho's mouth was dry, and he knew it was a good sign that he shouldn't say anything. But he'd never had much sense of self-preservation. "I do remember it," he whispered hoarsely. "I do ask myself."

Wade's nod was slow. "Good," he finally said, and then he started down the path again, but stopped maybe ten paces away. "You're not so pure, Jay Crewe," he called back. "And I'm not quite as far gone as you think."

There was something burbling up inside Jericho, something that made no damn sense. But he knew what it was, and he was tired of lying to himself. Standing there in the forest, drenched in fast-cooling sweat and staring down at Wade fucking Granger, he felt an undeniable sense of hope. "Not that far gone?" he said. "Prove it!"

Wade looked back up at him, and after a moment's thought, he gave Jericho a smile. A real, pure, affectionate grin. "Maybe I will," he shouted, and he turned and headed out of the forest.

Explore more of the *Common Law* series at:
riptidepublishing.com/titles/series/common-law

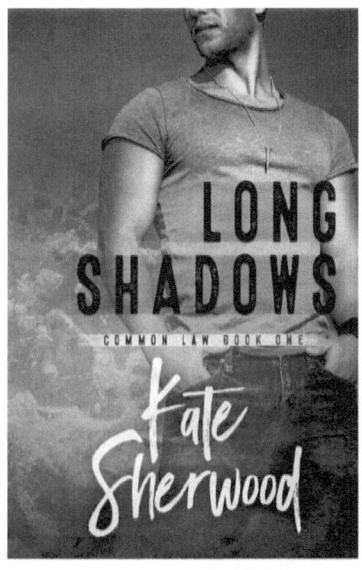

Dear Reader,

Thank you for reading Kate Sherwood's *Embers*!

We know your time is precious and you have many, many entertainment options, so it means a lot that you've chosen to spend your time reading. We really hope you enjoyed it.

We'd be honored if you'd consider posting a review—good or bad—on sites like **Amazon, Barnes & Noble, Kobo, Goodreads, Twitter, Facebook, Tumblr,** and your blog or website. We'd also be honored if you told your friends and family about this book. Word of mouth is a book's lifeblood!

For more information on upcoming releases, author interviews, blog tours, contests, giveaways, and more, please sign up for our weekly, spam-free newsletter and visit us around the web:

Newsletter: tinyurl.com/RiptideSignup
Twitter: twitter.com/RiptideBooks
Facebook: facebook.com/RiptidePublishing
Goodreads: tinyurl.com/RiptideOnGoodreads
Tumblr: riptidepublishing.tumblr.com

Thank you so much for Reading the Rainbow!

RiptidePublishing.com

ABOUT THE

AUTHOR

Kate Sherwood started writing about the same time she got back on a horse after almost twenty years away from riding. She'd like to think she was too young for it to be a midlife crisis, but apparently she was ready for some changes!

Kate grew up near Toronto, Ontario, and went to school in Montreal, then Vancouver. But for the last decade or so she's been a country girl. Sure, she misses some of the conveniences of the city, but living close to nature makes up for those lacks. She's living in Ontario's "cottage country"—other people save up their time and come to spend their vacations in her neighborhood, but she gets to live there all year round!

Since her first book was published in 2010, she's kept herself busy with novels, novellas, and short stories in almost all the subgenres of m/m romance. Contemporary, suspense, sci-fi, or fantasy—the settings are just the backdrop for her characters to answer the important questions: How much can they share, and what do they need to keep? Can they bring themselves to trust someone, after being disappointed so many times? Are they brave enough to take a chance on love?

Kate's books balance drama with humor, angst with optimism. They feature strong, damaged men who fight themselves harder than they fight anyone else. And, wherever possible, there are animals: horses, dogs, cats ferrets, squirrels . . . sometimes it's easier to bond with a nonhuman, and most of Kate's men need all the help they can get.

With her writing, Kate is still learning, still stretching herself, and still enjoying what she does. She's looking forward to sharing a lot more stories in the future. (And check out her imaginary friend, Cate Cameron, who writes m/f romance and YA.)

Visit Kate at katesherwoodbooks.com or facebook.com/kate. sherwood.79, or Tweet away at twitter.com/kate_sherwood.

Enjoy more stories like
Embers
at RiptidePublishing.com!

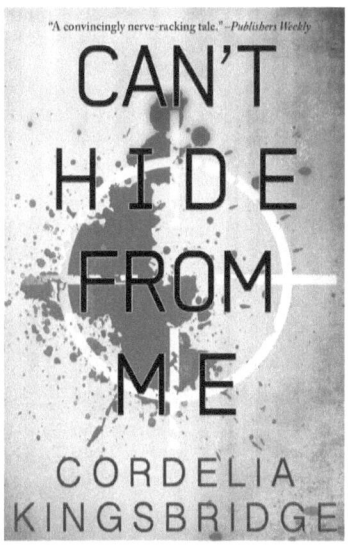

Friendly Fire
ISBN: 978-1-62649-482-4

Can't Hide From Me
ISBN: 978-1-62649-444-2

Earn Bonus Bucks!

Earn 1 Bonus Buck for each dollar you spend. Find out how at
RiptidePublishing.com/news/bonus-bucks.

Win Free Ebooks for a Year!

Pre-order coming soon titles directly through our site and you'll
receive one entry into a drawing for a chance to win free books for
a year! Get the details at RiptidePublishing.com/contests.